A

RAZOR'S EDGE OF

REVENGE II

~ A DOUBLE EDGE BLADE ~

Taboo

Also by the Author;

A Victims of Justice

A Razor's Edge of Revenge

A Struggling Soul

A Message to my Teenage Self

A Victim in Thug Mansion

"A Razor's Edge of Revenge II"
- Taboo
"Free Taboo Publishing LLC."
Copyright © 2024

ISBN: 978-1-963855-01-2

Preface

In no way does this author or Free Taboo Publishing, LLC. wish to glorify or promote gangs, drugs, or violence. Kids should take it as a warning, of what could happen, as well as what those consequences can be, and adults should teach the kids to avoid drugs, and gang activity, and to know the value of life. Do not throw your life away. All life is precious.

That being said, this book is a work of art, fiction, and meant to be entertainment. None of the people or names are real, nor are they intended to resemble anyone in real life. It does include real places to make it more real, as well as some real situations. It is FACTS that Congress has passed the First Step Act bill that takes the stacking out of the 924(c) stacking law, yet they consciously made the decision to allow all of those sentenced under this draconian law to stay imprisoned under this outdated and unfair sentencing enhancement. There are tens of thousands of people sentenced to hundreds of years, just like this author is currently sentenced to 91 years for non-violent, victimless drug and gun possession charges.

The current average federal sentence for murder is 22 years. This author was sentenced to over four times the national average federal murder sentence. Just for possession of things. Not for anything violent. Not for any victims. Not for using the guns. He could have committed four murders and gotten less time.

Our sitting congress this year, 2022, has the SAFE Justice Act, the First Step Implementation Act, and many more bills for criminal justice reform just on hold in front of them. We need Congress to act NOW! Stop these unfair and ridiculous sentences! I encourage all of you who believe that the 851 and 924(c) laws are unfair to call or write to your Congressman and ask them to pass these bills! Ask for a change in this Criminal INjustice System!

TABOO

Dedicated to...

To my son Anselmo, "Sammy".

Only 16, but already a better man than I could ever be.

I love you.

Acknowledgement

All thanks to my Lord Jesus Christ above all else. Also, to my readers and fans who are in love with my work and support my dreams. To MoneyRed for all the help with this book. A special thanks to Ruth Okocha for all her efforts towards editing this and 'A Victim of Justice' and putting them together gracefully. Also to the graphic designer who does an amazing job! My mom Kathy and stepdad Dave Evans, for raising my son to be a good person. To Lindsey for raising my daughter, you've always had my heart, and always will. My sister Laurie, for always being there for me. Mike Lee for ridin' this bid with me. Shane and Travis Stubblefield, my brothers from another mother.

Thanks to Vini for pushing me to achieve my goals and her artistic influences on me, and for being a great friend. My family Big Eric, Lil' Eric, and Mikey. Kira and Bella, Nichole Criss, Desiree Locke, and Chad Lobsinger. Dina for always making me smile.

To Carmen and Melissa Bezares, Bladimir, and Roger. Alyssa McCown for all your support on this bid! Fransisco and Jessica Alejandro, Kristi and Michelle "Momsdukes" Warner, Breanna Klein, Momo, Niki Hill, Craig Williams, Janel, Heather Campbell, Tiffany, Tammy, Cassie Cabrera, Tasha Diaz, Zack, Fallon, Laura

Mathis, Ivy, Rico, Lori & Athena Bailey, Ena Weeks, Brandi Carter, Randy Abott, Budda, Miss Cheryl Yeary-Eisen, Jamie & Debbie Barrow, Natalie, Brat, Stephanie & Nicole Lewis, Stephan & Livi Smith, Paulie, Samantha, and all of the homies in the Penitentiary: To my friend and colleague D.C. Redz, and MoneyRed. To Kic-Doe, Kojac, Dizzy, Chance, Bankroll, Money Mark, Gutta, Al, Revenue, Fat, Tay, Fruit, Checkmate, AP, Bogie, Zoe, Tank, Iceman, Run-Run, D, Truly, O, Herb, Nard, Cheeks.

To all the dead homies, gone but not forgotten: Savannah Balcom, (who saved my life when I got shot 3 times), My father Mike Yeary, Jovan 'Wolf' Gomez, Chris 'Chuck' Waters, Leighton Peale, Todd Reynalds, Christian '561' Scott, Eugene 'Chico' Simon, Manuel 'Slim' Valbueno, Jaime Medina, Paul 'Big Daddy' Martinez, Charlie Kline, Dave Barrow, Charlie Shultz, Miss Debbie Yeary, Brandon Gilcher, Tenesha Faria, Rick Marsh, and Maria Castro.

To Congress: Thank you for passing the First Step Act, so my 91-year sentence for non-violent, victimless crimes has now been illegal for 4 years, we need for you to make it retroactive! Pass the SAFE Justice Act immediately!

To the best lawyer besides Mike Salnick, my guy Mike Smith who fought like hell to give back these 91 years, even though we lost I loved his fight! Good guy!

Prologue

Dice and his group are facing the front of Grove Custom Auto. They've been sitting in stolen cars, parked across the street in the post office employee parking lot since 9am. Kilo was sweating a little bit in anticipation, and trying to will Sin and Sike to show themselves so he can send them back to their maker just as quickly.

Kilo knew that the Big Homie Gunz and his soldiers are out back in between the garage bays and small businesses trying to blend in. They would catch any of these cockroaches when they scurry out the back, trying to escape the overwhelming warfare that ZMA are waging in the front of the mechanic's building.

Luna and her team from Tamarind Avenue, Downtown, were split between the South and North sides of the building, in case any roaches were able to escape out of the barred up windows. Since once the shooting starts, all the teams would converge on the building in full force, Gunz having given the order to leave nothing in their place breathing, there would be no chance for anyone to get away anyways, plus Kilo was out for blood and wouldn't stop until they payed for crossing him.

Quan sat next to Kilo in the back of the Ford Explorer that Glizzy had stolen from the longterm parking lot at Palm Beach International Airport earlier in the morning. This would be Quan's first time putting in work, yet he seemed uncharacteristically calm and focused. He is comfortable. It was at that moment that a Cadillac Escalade pulled up with Sin driving and two of his shooters in the shotgun and passenger seat positions, getting out of the truck together.

Kilo started, but Dice grabbed his leg, staying him. "Everyone hold positions, we waiting on the birthday boy to show to his party, and yep, that's him pulling up now, a'ight y'all, let's go get these hoe ass paintchos!"

As the nigga, Sike, got out of the 1985 box Chevy Caprice, he looked around nervously, before continuing inside the opened garage bay door. As soon as his back was to them, all of the ZMA soldiers rushed towards the building after him, right on his heels.

Kilo's anticipation and Quan's loyalty to Kilo, had put them in front of the rest of the older gangstas, as their athleticism had taken over, their highly conditioned football player legs running faster than anyone else. As they ran, Kilo lifted his machine pistol at the first target he should have already killed, yet had let make it.

His mistake had brought them all here.

Sike turned just in time to lock eyes with his killer, as Kilo lifted his MAC-10 and opened fire, turning Sike's white Tee into a tie-dye shirt, as about 10 holes appeared on it, turning it different shades of red. He was dead before he hit the dirty shop floor, already a memory.

As Kilo slowed down, reveling in his sweet revenge, another short burst of rounds exploded right next to him. Quan.

Tatatatatatatat! Tat! Tat! Tatatatat!

A Skinny Cuban had popped up to his left from nearby the cash register, just lifting his big chrome Barretta 9mm when Quan has saved Kilo, opening fire on him, and ending his life with a vertical line of shots from his chest, going through his chest, going through his neck and finally, a head shot.

Kilo took it upon himself to start duck-walking towards the office. Shots came within inches of his head and one even hit his left shoulder. He saw the big Cuban with face tats coming out of the office door in slow motion and a smoking gun dropping his magazine out of its handle, his intention to replace it with a new magazine. Kilo raised his MAC and unloaded with about 15 of his remaining rounds, ending him. Kilo ejected his empty mag and slid in his only spare, ready again.

Shots continued to ring out as Kilo creeped into the office hallway separating the front desk from the manager's office, from where the big Cuban had popped out of. A flash of a face with braids on his head popped back behind the door, thinking Kilo didn't see him.

Kilo approached the already ajar door cautiously. He couldn't hold back anymore, thinking the best way to flush a rat is with brute force, not cheese. He kicked the open door as hard as he could, hearing a grunt and a low crunch in the same split second before he let a spray of rounds loose, pointing downwards, intending to maim, not kill.

"Arg-ahh! Mothafucka!" shouted Sin's voice.

Kilo bent around the broken office door that Sin had been trying to use to catch Kilo slipping, in an attempt to hide behind it and catch him off guard. He was able to smile at the sight before him: Sin on the dirty floor, knees both shattered by his busted knee caps, from the damage of Kilo's bullets, and his broken nose gushing from the kicking of the door into his face.

"You got away the first time bitch-ass nigga, but I knew you would fall into my hands eventually! Karma's a bitch, ain't she, Sin?" Kilo asks quietly and reserved, as if he was born to do this.

"Lil' fucking Maniac, huh?" asks Sin, giving an evil and resigned smile through the pain, playing it down, so as not to appear weak.

"-the fuck you smiling at, fool? I'm 'bout to send you to hell-" started Kilo.

"I'm laughing cuz you ain't know what really brought us here to this moment! How you think I even met Maniac? I'm from out West! I knew I shoulda searched that house that day! She ain't tell me y'all was home, that's how you knew it was me-"

"She? She-who, nigga? You're a fucking liar!" screamed Kilo as he shoots Sin in the knee cap again, splattering blood everywhere, along with some of his bone fragments, Kilo was amazed that he was still conscious through this type of pain.

Sin started to laugh at him, as he knew it was all over for him.

"Nah, not your moms, jit. Your 'Aunt Nikki'! She introduced me to your pops! And I fucked them all!" Sin started laughing again. "I killed your dad, fucked your moms, and even put 'Aunt Nikki' in your-"

Tat! Tatat! Tatatatat! Tat! Tat!

"Die, mother fucker!" screamed Kilo, squeezing his finger again and again, the firing pin landing on an empty chamber.

Click! Click! Click! Click! Click! Click!

§§§§

"Die, mother fucker-Die, mother fucker-Die-"

"Kian!" yelled Isabella, shaking Kilo awake as he was having a bad dream again. The bad dream. The dream that wasn't actually a dream, but instead, a memory.

"Shit. Sorry, bae...I was having that dream again..."

4

"It's okay, baby. Are you alright?" she asked, always so full of concern for him.

"Yea, bae. I'm cool. Sorry I fell asleep again. I should get going before your dad gets home from his shift," said Kilo, starting to get up.

Isabella looked at her clock on her in-table and reached for Kilo, stopping him. She turned her big beautiful green eyes up to him under sleepy eye lashes. "He doesn't get off for another hour," she said.

A knowing smile on his face, Kilo bent down and kissed her beautiful pouty lips as she pulled him back into the bed, onto her. Kissing him, she reached below and guided him inside of her, filling her, loving her. As always, completing her.

Still kissing, Kilo slowly stroked Isabella until her moans became louder and desperate. "Aww, baby. You always feel so good..." moaned Isabella.

Kilo stroked her lovingly, instead of violently as they sometimes did when frantically trying to bring each other to climax. Being in love with Isabella, he wanted to show her as she always showed him by her selflessness and kindness. She had been with him over two years now, since 9th grade and he had felt something special about her since day one. Since the first minute.

Kilo looked into her eyes as they made love. She was so perfect, so damn beautiful inside and out, that he couldn't see what she saw in him but he was grateful for her. As Kilo stroked Isabella, she began to pull on his ass, biting her bottom lip and closing her pretty eyes, a sign he knew all too good. He sped up his pace.

"'Yes, baby! You know my body so good! Make me come, baby!" she moaned.

"You always so perfect, baby! Your pussy so damn good, Izzy! You got me ready to buss, baby! Damn!" grunted Kilo, now pushing in and out of Isabella faster and creating a puddle under them on the bedsheets.

"Cum for me, Kian! I'm ready, bae! Come with me!" screamed Isabella.

Knowing his communicating with her was the best way to control her orgasms, he delayed just long enough to climax with her, which was their favorite way to make love. "When, baby? When you want me to come?" he asked, speeding up even faster while being even more turned on, finally ready to bust with her.

"'Now! Baby! Come now! I'm-ah! Ah! I'm-come-ing!"

"I'm coming with you baby! Ah!" said Kilo, letting loose inside of his girl's amazing and gushy pussy.

"Oh! Baby! We're coming-together!" she screamed. "I-I-love you-Kian! I-love-you!"

"I love you too, Izzy! Damn..." said Kilo, laying on top of her, still inside of her, yet too spent to withdraw.

Looking into his eyes, Isabella was lost in him. She adored him, yet really loved how much he adored her and showed his feelings by actions. "Baby?" she asked.

"Yea?"

"Do you think we'll always be together?" she asked, serious.

"I know we will..." answered Kilo.

"How do you know?"

"Because," he said, starting to drift off. "You're my piece..."

"Your piece?" she demanded with attitude, misunderstanding him. "What are you talking about, Kian?"

"What I mean is: A puzzle can only fit a certain way. Each piece can only fit where it goes. So, Imani, Jay, Quan and my moms all surround *my* puzzle piece. They fit. You can put a thousand pieces in that last missing spot, but only ONE piece will fit. That's you. You're my piece, Isabella. No other piece can fit, no matter how hard you force it..."

"I am so in love with you, Kian..." said Isabella, almost falling asleep with an angelic smile on her pretty face.

"And I - you, bae...But I need to go 'fore ya dad catch us and kill me..."

Chapter One

Nikki

Two Years Ago

Nikki stuck her acrylic pinkie nail inside the little apple 15X15 8-ball sized coke baggie to get another bump as she sat back philosophizing on the evils in life and how karma was such a motherfucker - yet the sister of life at the same time. Both of them bitches.

Everything that she had done had inadvertently caused her best friend, Skyla, to suffer through what has now befallen her in a mean and twisted kind of evil fate. Did she really deserve this? she asks herself. She thinks back to when it all had started back when she had introduced Maniac to a few of her people from The City. Carol City. Which is now called Miami Gardens.

Things had gotten out of hand. She can admit that now, but it hadn't been remotely her fault. One night 13 years earlier, after a night out at KOD, or King of Diamonds as it is known in Miami, where she had introduced Maniac to her Haitian Sensations friend-Lemonhead, out of Lil Haiti, she and Maniac had hooked up. *Really* hooked up.

She knew it had been so wrong, her being his wife's best friend, but Skyla has always bragged about how happy she was, how well he treated her and how amazing the sex was between them. That had made the curiosity begin to blossom inside of Nikki until she finally couldn't help herself and acted upon it. A little bit tipsy herself, she took advantage of Maniac's drunken state, seducing him and putting that pussy on him until they both awoke the next day, foggy and hungover.

Her friend Skyla had not been underestimating Maniac's pipe game. The nigga could literally lay it down and put a bitch to sleep. But to her, it started to feel like something more than that though, as Nikki was beginning to fall in love with Maniac while she was introducing him to all of her contacts. After her father had been murdered in Overtown almost three years before, leaving her with all the contracts-yet no hustle game to take over her father's empire in Miami Gardens housing projects, formally known as Carol City Haitian Cartel, she had decided to link Maniac up and take a little cut.

Falling for Maniac had been the biggest mistake of her life though. She had put herself out there one night and he had literally laughed in her face. Then it had gotten even worse, even more painful for her, so bad in fact, that she still winced in pain at the thought.

"Bitch - are you fucking crazy? I'm not leaving my fucking wife for you! I fucked you one time! And that was *only* cuz I was drunk and fucked up... I would never leave Sky! For you or any other bitch on God's green earth. Never ..." said Maniac vehemently.

"Baby, I'm pregnant! What are you saying?" asked a desperate and crying Nikki, not understanding at all what was happening and feeling degraded.

"What I'm saying..." started Maniac as he counted out a stack of $100's. "Is...take care of it, Nikki. We ain't all that. I'm never going to be with you!"

He gave her $2,300 and asked her to go get an abortion. An abortion that she never did go and get, but yet, she allowed him to think that she did. She had concealed her pregnancy for her first 6 months, but then she ghosted for her third trimester, telling Skyla-and in turn, Maniac-that she went to rehab, as she was known to snort a lot of coke. But really she had went into hiding.

She had another surprise at the birth when Child Protective Services and DCF took her son, Emelio, because he had cocaine in his bloodwork-which had been taken after her labor without her knowledge, a common hospital practice. Things really turned around when her mother came to the rescue, filing paperwork and adopting him and raising him as her grandson, with Nikki moving in there with them, being a constant part in his life.

After all she had been through and the way that she had been treated by Maniac, she would never forgive, never forget. She had changed completely. No longer soft or tenderhearted. She had turned coldhearted. Mean even. Cynical. She would be sure to get even - to show him the razor's edge of her revenge, but she would bid her time. She would set him up to be killed and then take over his flourishing drug business with prejudice and set it up for her son to take over, becoming the real 'Kingmaker' in the dope game. She finally found her inner gangsta.

But years had ended up passing. In fact, her best friend, Skyla, ended up having her second son, Jermaine, only six months after Nikki had Emelio. She faked tears of joy for her friend, but in reality, she was crying tears of a broken heart. She and her son, Emelio, had been rejected, while Maniac and Skyla had two princes: Kian, the oldest; and then Jermaine. Nikki planned to get even. If it was the last thing she would do, she would see the two little princes fatherless, while her own prince would take over what she builds with a new king. A temporary king. Ultimately, a means to an end.

Sin enters the picture.

They set it all up together. Emelio was already 12 when Sin had killed Maniac. They had been on the right path to getting to the bag until Sin had unexpectedly started using a different plug. This 'Cien Fuegos', a Y-Lo associate of his from Cuba, was a problem.

She couldn't figure out what the fuck had went so wrong with her plan or why Sin had deviated from it, but to make matters worse, Nikki couldn't make Sin fall in love with her either. No matter how hard she tries or how many different sexual favors she was doing. Dirty shit, too. He just won't wifey her.

She began to wonder what was so wrong with her. She was every man's dream, a Halle Berry look-a-like, just blessed with beautiful ebony skin instead of red-boned. Plus, she goes both ways and has been giving him three-some after three-some in an attempt to please him. She even gave him a three-some with Skyla, the wife of the man he had just killed. What could be a better turn-on than that? she asks herself. Nothing is, that's what! It turns her on just thinking about it.

But then, the reality of what the the news that she just received means for her plans for Emelio: She's got to start all over again. Sin was killed in a shoot-out after being brutally tortured for some reason. But after being in his S550 Benz with him and being shot at, she thinks she might have a clue into who might have been responsible. But her son was only 13! He wasn't ready to get into the game yet or take his rightful place as Prince Maniac and take over the streets!

Or was he? she asks herself. No. He isn't. But.

It doesn't matter to her if he is ready or not, it's all going to be on his shoulders now, whether he is ready for it or not. He ain't gon' be the one with greatness thrust upon him, she thought to herself, he's the one that's gonna *become* great and build the whole empire for them to take over South Florida. Her plans would come into fruition, she just had to start his training now, and she knew just who to call: Haitian Sensations Lemonhead.

Chapter Two

Present Day

Emelio

"C'mon, lil nigga! Just like I taught ya! That's right!" said Calico-Zoe, rooting for Lil E as he is boxing an older and larger kid right outside Edison Projects, off of Northwest 68th Street and 4th Court, a trapping spot in Lil Haiti, which is a dangerous hood in Northwest Miami. A crowd is starting to form around the boys fighting. The much younger Lil E had been training hard most of his life, and it's beginning to show in his fighting style, as he is not only bobbing and weaving like a champ, but also parrying and being more patient, landing better and more aggressive body blows combined with clean and more effective uppercuts. Big Kev, the larger and older 17 year old kid he is fighting, was about 6 foot and 190 pounds, while Emelio, known as Lil E, at 15 now, is only 5'9 and 160 pounds soaking wet. It didn't even faze Lil E in the least bit. This is the reason he had been training so hard: To win. To demolish his opponent. To take over and become the King of the Streets, just as his mother had always taught him, he would do. She said his father had been the HNIC, or Head Nigga In Charge of Palm Beach County and that he would still be running shit if he hadn't been killed in the dope game by the Y-Lo's, a murderous Miami street gang that had clout as well as shooters. Thus his fighting, training and then fighting some more. Not only would he be able to take his rightful place as heir to the throne, but he would avenge his father, Maniac's murder by finding the head of the Y-Los and killing him, and any other Y-Lo that came into contact with him, getting in his way. But first he had to earn his place, his position. Big Kev was already getting tired, and Lil E can sense it. Big Kev's long reach is being limited by Lil E's continued invasions into his personal space. Lil E was dropping left hook and

12

right hand uppercut combinations before backing up with a couple of left jabs to keep Big Kev's long reach from connecting. It was working and it was devastating to Big Kev's defenses.

Having had enough of Lil E's hands, Big Kev suddenly dropped his head and rushed at Lil E, thinking that he can use his size to bully Lil E and overpower him. It would've worked on most of these lil niggas in Lil Haiti, but not with Lil E. He is of a different caliber. He is trained for this shit.

Lil E simply lowered his center of gravity while simultaneously bringing his right knee up to connect with Big Kev's wide nose, creating a blood fountain and shocking Big Kev immediately upon seeing the amount of blood that was coming from his face, which was something new to Big Kev, him being known as a Lil Haiti knockout artist, infamous in Miami Edison Senior High School over on 62nd Street. His hands went involuntarily to his nose, leaving the rest unprotected.

His hands went involuntarily to his nose, leaving the rest unprotected. Lil E immediately took advantage: Left jab, right cross, and a final left hook, folding Big Kev into a sack-a-potatoes on the floor, literally knocked unconscious and hurt bad. Lil E walked around the big kid, looking each and every one of Big Kev's homies dead in their eyes before laughing. "So you puss-ass niggas want my lunch money? C'mon! Who's next?" he asked, as he suddenly turned around and viciously tried to kick a field goal through Big Kev's front teeth, kicking him in the mouth as hard as he possibly could, breaking his jaw and cracking his skull on the concrete. Big Kev's condition didn't visually change at first, he was still bleeding everywhere and still on roll-call in Dreamland, most likely concussed and in an immediate coma.

"Bunch a hoes!" said Lil E, turning his back on the older kids, bending down and rifling through Big Kev's pockets. He pulled out a roll of $1s and $5s, what was most likely all the other kids at school's lunch money that Big Kev had forcefully taken, being a bully that he is known to be.

"Two things about a bully," said Lil E as he turned to face the rest of the crowd, acting like a college professor, even pausing in the right places to create a dramatic moment in his oration. "It's all fun and games- till someone gets hurt." He pointed at Kev's form and did his dramatic pause for effect again, then added, "And it ain't no fun when the rabbit got the gun, now is it, Big Kev?"

Lil E, still holding the money he pulled from Big Kev's pockets in his hand, looked down at Big Kev, all eyes followed his. Big Kev was choking on his own blood everywhere. He was dying. His body started convulsing, the brain trauma just too much.

"OH MY GOD! Call an ambulan-" started a woman, moving toward Big Kev, before Calico-Zoe stepped right in front of her, blocking her way.

"You tryna be next, bitch?" asked Calico-Zoe, with a vicious and merciless smile stretching his whole face in an invitation to a personal hell that he would just love to deliver to her. As she backed away, Lil E turned again to Big Kev's homies, a look of utter horror and shock uniformly decorating all of their faces. "Y'all boys tryna get down? Who's next?" he asked, still like the devil at a mass genocide.

All eyes turned back down to Big Kev, who chose that moment to stop convulsing, coughed a few times and laid motionless. He had stopped breathing, and if that wasn't enough of a sign, the sound of his bowels letting lose completed the reality for all of those watching, being witnesses to a man dying. Or a kid dying, if you considered the oversized bully as a kid.

"OH MY GOD!" yelled the same woman, now running away, not wanting to see any more. Lil E only smiled once more, then turned away, having caught the attention of all the former bully's friends, letting them know by his smile. He might only be 15, but this still wasn't his first body. Hell, this wasn't his first body just from using his hands. His first body, at the tender age of 12, had been from choking out a kid who had called him "a bastard with no daddy". That was before Lemonhead's rigorous training, before he had went on the run, had started fucking with his mother and taking Lil E under his wing. Before Calico-Zoe had ended up as his almost-step-daddy, training him even more. Now he has, not only a purpose in life, but also some focus and a goal to pursue: taking over his father's abandoned streets. Click! Clack!

Calico-Zoe had pulled out his all chromed-out Draco and held it threateningly up after racking the bolt, putting one in the chamber, as well as putting everyone on notice that he is dead serious about Lil E and keeping his name out of their mouths.

"Need I say more?" asked Calico-Zoe aggressively. "I don't give a fuck about how shit go down in the rest of Dade County, but here in Lil Haiti? We don' talk to police! Same day ya ass be on First 48, same day ya ass *be* First 48, ya feel me?"

He needn't have asked. Memories of the dead body fresh in their minds, but the memory of who had actually done it was already fading from their memory banks.

Chapter Three

Miami, Florida

- Nikki -

These last two years since her coming back to Miami and moving to the Edison Projects, first with Lemonhead and finally with Calico-Zoe, had been trying and had changed Nikki beyond her expectations. First her treatment by Maniac, DCF's involvement in her life with her son, the back to back loss of Maniac, her father, and finally Sin, all added up and had turned her into a demon.

Gone was the sweet and sexually expressive Nikki, just trying to have fun, get drunk and high, then fuck. She is all about business now. All about money now. All she wants now is for her son to take her bloodline and Maniac's old hustle to all new levels. She is all about a means to an end, so if it wasn't making them no dollars, it sure as fuck don't make no sense. It is all about her son now. All about proving that he is better than Carol City's Haitian Cartel; better than Maniac, and especially better than her.

Her thoughts were suddenly interrupted as she is sitting at Jack & Jill's hair salon over on Northwest 64th and 2nd Avenue, Monique just finishing up with her new real human hair weave, leaving it wavy and flowing down her back to her perfect apple bottom, her nails having already been done and on fleek. She is already looking ghetto fabulous and feeling herself. As she is just about to get up, her back to the front door, yet still always on point in the mirror, Jah'Quesha, a known hood gossip, runs into the shop.

"Monique! Girl you neva gon' believe what just happen'! That lil evil jit, Lil E just be done killed Big Kev down 4th court and-" Jah'Quesha had started before she froze, mid-statement after seeing Monique's eyes darting all around and then down at the

16

chair in front of her, whose occupant is not visible to Jah'Quesha's view since her back is turned.

That all changed in an instant, and it seems as though all the air is sucked out of the room, the tension so thick it could dull a razor's edge in attempt of cutting it. Ever so slowly, the chair in front of Monique begins to turn toward the direction of the intruder, deliberately delaying the climax, causing even more of a dramatic scene while raising Jah'Quesha's anxiety levels to an unbelievable all time high, her blood pressure through the roof.

"I...ah, I mean...ah-" started Jah'quesha, in some unfamiliar way of an apology attempt or acceptance of responsibility. But she is unexpectedly cut off.

"Bitch, continue...You was just saying something about my son?" asked Nikki, slowly and deliberately enunciating each syllable. Her body was moving slower than anyone thought even possible, like the uncoiling of a wild and dangerous snake, ready to strike, knowing it's prey can't escape its wrath, yet taking time and drawing out the coming meal already in its grasp, toying with it.

"I meant no disrespect, ah, I...I mean..." Jah'Quesha trailed off, now completely lost on what more she could possibly say.

"I'm listening..." said Nikki, taking another incredibly slow step toward her prey, her slow movements concealing the fact that she's slowly taken three steps closer to Jah'Quesha, all with the slowness of a turtle.

Finally, snapping out of the daze that Nikki's lazy movement had her in and realizing that Nikki had been moving slowly toward her all the while, she dropped all pretenses of dignity or facade of a gangsta-ass hood rat and Jah'Quesha took off, sprinting out the same door that she just had run into.

Nikki's reaction was immediate and absolute. Running after Jah'Quesha, she caught her in between a Lexus truck and a bubble Chevy Caprice on "26s. With her right hand full of hair, she jerked back, yanking Jah'Quesha's wig right off her bald head covered in a stocking cap. With her left hand reached out, she quickly gripped Jah'Quesha's shirt. She stopped in her tracks, yanking her shirt and causing Jah'Quesha's legs to go out from under her as she's slammed flat on her back onto the concrete in between the two cars, her head right next to the rear passenger side "26 inch Lexani rim on the Chevy.

Nikki punched her in the eye hard.

"So, what was you saying about my son, bitch?" asked Nikki, pushing Jah'Quesha's face into the tire and rim right next to her head.

"'Nothing! I said nothing! I ain't say shit, I swear!" shouted Jah'Quesha as all of the other ladies began to come outside and watch the spectacle, no sympathy written in any of their faces. Everyone of them knowing the rules in Edison PJs. You don't talk shit about a bitch's kids, even bad-ass jits like Emelio. Especially Emelio, since he's a grandson to Carol City's Haitian Cartel, but especially since he's the notoriously violent Nikki Lewis' kid.

"Oh, shit. My bad, girl! I must have heard you wrong!" said Nikki, feigning gullibility, as if she actually didn't hear Jah'Quesha's mouth actually say what she'd said.

"Ah...Yea, I wasn't ...I was talking about somebody else, Nikki. You know I would never talk bad about your boy..." said Jah'Quesha, relieved that Nikki believed her and was backing off a little bit, allowing her to start getting up as Nikki stood up.

Turning over on her hands and knees, just starting to get up and right herself, she never saw it coming. She sure felt the blow to her head, though. Quarters went flying everywhere as she saw a

18

sock with a hole in it hanging from Nikki's hand, having come from no where.

"Puss-ass bitch! Don't nobody believe all of that shit! Bitch, you actin' like all us wasn't just in there, hearing what you said!" Nikki said, opening her arms to indicate all of the other women from the salon currently locked in on their dramatic confrontation, enjoying all the theatrics, especially the sock filled with quarters trick.

"I... I'm...I'm sorry, I..." she says and falls back down, face back down and next to the rim.

Nikki immediately dropped the sock and gripped Jah'Quesha by the back on her neck, pulling her face toward the chrome Lexani rim. "Okay, you're sorry! Okay, I guess that fixes everything then, don't it? Well, bitch, since you like to keep names in ya mouth so damn much... BITCH-Open ya mouth-" yelled Nikki, roughly leading Jah'Quesha's face-and in particularly- her mouth against the lip of the rim, right where the tire meets the metal rim.

"Bitch! *Open* ya mouth!" screams NIkki, throwing her face repeatedly against the metal of the rim, then finally forcing her fingers into Jah'Quesha's mouth to open the gossiping jaws of this hood-rat-busy-body-bitch.

"Okay now! That's enough!" says a woman in the crowd, trying to calm Nikki-and in turn, the whole theatrical event, down. But one look from a deadly serious Nikki ends any further protests from taking place, from her or any other onlookers.

"Ahh-arg! Arg! Ahh!" Jah'Quesha's frantic pleas are garbled by her mouth being forced to bite down on the lip of the rim and tire as Nikki holds her head in the exact position she wants it in to maximize the point she is trying to make.

With Jah'Quesha's top teeth on the lip of the rim and her bottom teeth biting down on the tough rubber of the low profile tire, Nikki puts her whole show into action, having the whole salon and now the entire plaza's attention on her carefully orchestrated event.

"Since you like keepin' names in that big-ass mouth of yours! Take a mouth fulla Lexani! Talk about Lexani next time you fix ya mouth to say anything out the way bout us and ours!" screamed Nikki before she stomped the back of Jah'Quesha's head into the Lexani rim.

"AHHH! AARGG! GGGRRR!" screamed Jah'Quesha, right before fainting, her broken jaw hanging sideways, blood draining out of her ruined mouth, almost all of her front teeth gone, three of the bottom teeth stuck in the tire as air is seeping out of the holes the teeth created through the hard rubber. The sight alone had made a few women sick, never seeing that kind of violence before, even living in Edison PJs.

"I bet next time ya ass be more careful who name you got in ya mouth, bitch! It betta be 'Lexani' and not none of me and mines..." Nikki said to the unconscious form of Jah'Quesha, then allowed her gaze to fall on the rest of the crowd. Some of whom were holding up cameras, filming the whole episode for kicks.

"That goes for the rest of you bitches, too! I bet' not see any video of this shit on any socials, or you already know who finna come and take them down...along with your whole family-down to the pitbull...play if ya want to..." Nikki added, before turning around as if not a care in the world, until she got to her truck, a black Genesis GV70. Noticing her broken nail she had just got done with Chinese acrylic claws and painted to perfection.

Her blood was boiling already because she couldn't overlook the fact of the story Jah'Quesha had burst in the beauty parlor screaming about and knowing there was some truth to it, but also because she had just spent four hours in Monique's shop and was still leaving with a broken nail.

Knowing that she didn't have the time to get it redone-and couldn't now at any rate with the scene she was now leaving behind her here, she lost her composure. "You! Broke! My! Nail!" she screamed, running back and giving Jah'Quesha a good kick in her stomach for each word she screamed aloud. Punishing her for not only breaking her nail, but for running her mouth, as much as for her being the bearer of bad news. Her son had killed again. He is just as she made him: a cold and calculating killer-soon to be gangsta. Soon to be Carol City Haitian Cartel heir.

Getting into her V70 on 26 inch Asanti faces, she peeled out of the plaza lot, just as a Jackson Memorial Hospital ambulance was pulling in to try and save Jah'Quesha's jaw. They needn't have rushed, as her jaw would surely be wired shut for 6 months, before she would even be able to see a dental surgeon about all of her broke and missing teeth.

§§§§

"Boy! The fuck I done tol' you about making a damn spectacle out of your self and drawing attention? I gotta hear about this dumbass shit at the fucking hair salon? And you-" started Nikki, going in on both of her boys, her son, as well as her damn man-child ass husband.

"Girl, chill da fuck out! He just bein' a man! You wanted him to go take ova' da 561, right? So that's what him' doin'-" butts in Calico-Zoe.

"Real killers and gangstas move in violence and silence and-" starts Nikki.

"Now you quoting rap lyrics to me... "

"And that dumbass shit was fucking loud and uncoordinated!"

"Kind of like your lil' episode down at Jack & Jills fucking beauty shop, eh?" he calmly answered her back, knowing just how to handle his wife. "Don't worry. Nobody fa g'won say no-ting! These my fucking projects, I make sho don't nobody say shit, but don't eva' think ya got tings g'won and I ain't fa know bout it! I tole ya me cheri, I got chu!"

Nikki could do nothing more than smile in gratitude, as Calico has been there for her more than she could've ever expected him to be. She was really sad though, because now with her son putting another body in the dirt, in addition to her own little episode down at the salon and Emelio's training being pretty much complete, his being just shy of becoming an adult, it was about time that they moved on and went back to the five-six- ace. Back to Palm "Money" Beach County. It is long overdue.

"Zaddy, look...Remember when we first got together and I told you the story and what my plans were for Emelio and what we would have to go do one day?" asked Nikki.

"Yea, I know. And I'm already knowing what you finna say, Cheri, and it's all good. I feel he and I ain't trippin' on it, you go back to 561 and do what you gotta do and I just fa slide back and fort' to visit so I can keep control dem here in Edison, ya feel?" says Calico-Zoe, always having known that this day would come, just surprised at how fast time moves in this life, and regretful for having to be separated from his little foster family.

"Don't worry, Zaddy. It won't take too long, I've been planning for just this moment for over 15 years and I got what it takes to put my plan into full effect. You sho' you gonna be alright without us for a lil' while?"

"Just do what ya g'won do and come back to Zaddy, my Zoe Queen..." said Calico-Zoe, as he kisses her forehead, nose, and then lips lovingly. Saying goodbye.

"I will, Zaddy. You know I will... "

Chapter Four

Kilo

It's been almost two years since Kilo murdered Sin and made him feel that razor sharp edge of his revenge. This should have been over, it should have satiated Kilo's thirst for revenge against his father-Maniac's killer, but it didn't. All it did was drive Kilo deeper into the game, drive him further into an unattainable obsession over the other pieces to the puzzle. Aunt Nikki.

Sin might have been the gun that killed Maniac, but even as that was the case, Aunt Nikki had been the manicured finger that pulled the trigger. She had been the one that orchestrated the entire set-up from straight out the gate.

"C'mon, Kian! Two more reps," said Quan, Kilo's day-one nigga.

"GRRAAHHH! Fuck!" growled Kilo as he pushed up a simple 220 pounds on the shoulder press weight bench at World's Gym on Congress and Lantana Road. "It's just no fuckin' good, bruh. It ain't getting no better, Quan. That shit's over with. It's been two years and ain't healed yet-"

"So, yea-my nigga, let's just give up then," interrupted Quan, with a typical sarcastic rendition of feeling sorry for Kilo's gun shot wound hit shoulder, feigning excusing his giving up on Kilo's physical therapy.

About two years ago, when they ran down on their ops, some Y-Los in a Delray Beach mechanic shop, Grove Custom Auto, Kilo had been shot with a high caliber full metal jacketed round that in turn, literally ripped apart his left shoulder. Kilo, in fact, has good reason to be upset and sorry for himself since it has completely ruined any chance for him continuing in his football career as a

24

wide receiver. He can rarely catch the ball using his left, and when he does, it causes him so much pain that it's hardly worth the effort it required to accomplish.

"Man, fuck all that sarcastic shit, bruh. It ain't happening..." said Kilo, still catching his breath and trailing off, having accepted this fate with finality, yet still upset about the whole thing that happened.

"A'ight, that's enough for today, we'll get back to it next week," said Quan, trying to sound upbeat and keep Kilo's spirits high, yet still failing at it.

Kilo's phone suddenly started vibrating and alerting him to an incoming call. A call on his personal iPhone 15Pro, as opposed to his Android work phone, which could only mean one thing: It is something important and something personal. Not business.

"Yeo," answered Kilo upon identifying the caller as one of his big homies, Haze. A big homie that had been with the Zoe Mafia Affiliate Family since its foundation - along with Kilo's father, and OG Dice, back when they had all been just teenagers.

What Haze was telling Kilo in his ear had Kilo's heart rate accelerating more than his workout here at the gym. It was something he had been waiting two years to hear, and now he could barely contain himself. He said nothing at all, but then hit the 'End' icon on his screen and deliberately placed the phone very gently on the bench next to him.

"What's up, thug?" asked Quan, concerned about Kilo's reaction from receiving the call and whatever news he heard from the other end.

"It's Haze. He had a Zoe Pound contact in Lil' Haiti who sent him some info and a picture. He's sending it now-" Kilo started to explain, when his phone alerted him to an incoming message. A picture interrupted his explanation.

Quan leans over his day-one nigga and looks at the picture displayed on the screen. It depicts the image of a beautiful chocolate complexioned sista with short frosted banana curls looking like a darker, younger version of Halle Berry, but it wasn't her beauty but the man she was standing hugged up with that got the boys' attention. It was who she was and what she had done that commanded such scrutiny from them. It was a picture of Aunt Nikki standing next to Calico-Zoe, Zoe Pound's leader and Macka-Zoe's right hand man.

"Holy shit, Key! You know who that is with her?" asked Quan in wonderment.

"Yea. I do, bruh. But it don't change a mutha-fuckin' thang! She gotta die! If he standin' next to her and get hit, I can't help-"

"Key- that nigga is said to have had a gun battle by himself in Richmond Heights against like ten niggas and killed every last one of-" started Quan.

"I don't give a fuck!" screamed Kilo, interrupting Quan and drawing several stares from the other gym members trying to do their workout routines.

"Say less, my Z. You know I be with you either way-all I'm saying is take your time and let's get her dolo, ya feel?" said Quan, getting up now that their workout for the day was over, other more important things having taken precedence.

"He said she runnin' trap out dem' Edison Jets, so I doubt she be leavin' trap, but when she do, I'm finna body this puss-ass hoe for good..." said Kilo, referring to the Edison Projects, notorious in the Lil' Haiti area for the three M's: Mackin', Money, and Murders.

Quan just nodded his head in support, Kilo already knowing that Quan was going to have his back no matter what, having seen that much at Grove Custom Auto when he'd been shot. A Cuban Y-Lo had been spraying bullets and might have hit Kilo in the head, had Quan not fired when he did and killed the guy just as his bullets struck, one hitting Kilo in his left shoulder.

Quan had showed more than his heart on that day, he showed a dedication and a willingness to go hard for his day-one nigga and for ZMA. It was that day that Quan became an official ZMA shooter.

Chapter Five

Isabella

"Isabella Ann Perelli! Talk to me! What is wrong? Are you okay?" asked Isabella's father worrying as she is bent over the kitchen sink, vomiting her guts out, tears pouring down her face in desperation. Fear is written all over her face, but she tries to hide it.

"I'm fine, daddy. I'm just sick to my stomach and anxious about finals-"

"Izzy," says her father, her best friend, and favorite person in the whole world, his voice having softened, knowing he is wrapped around her little finger and adores her with all of his heart. "I'm just worried, Sweetheart. Let me take you in and run some tests."

Isabella's dad is a nurse at JFK Trauma Center, so the one thing she knows she can't do, is let him run any tests. The results would crush him. Especially since Isabella hasn't even turned 17 yet and has her whole life ahead of her. Or had, that is.

Isabella is an aspiring artist, and even her being only a junior, the Palm Beach School of the Arts has made many attempts to get Isabella to come to their institution for specialized help in developing creativity in her art and style. For the past two years, Isabella has flat out refused her father's pleas for her to go there, insisting on staying at John I. Leonard High School, the last six months of those two years, she has been hiding letters from them now, saying they can help her to get into the Rhode Island School of Design, known as RISD in the art world and most sought after college in the Northeast. A really big opportunity for her, and one that her dad would never allow her to pass up.

"Okay, Daddy. Maybe later, you know if I missed finals, it would destroy my 4.0 GPA and I've gotta keep it up to-"

"Fine, sweetheart. But don't make yourself sick with stress. I'm sure you'll do fine, baby. You always do," he said lovingly as he hugged her before kissing her on the forehead and grabbing his keys off of the kitchen counter. "I'll see you tonight?"

"Yes, Daddy. I'll be home after Kian's game," she replied.

"Right...Kian's game..." said her father as he walked off, mumbling discontentedly about how Kian had been monopolizing all of Isabella's time, taking her away from him. In reality, Kian hasn't played much in any of the games since his shoulder injury but still had to be there dressed out for the roster. "Wow, listen to me, calling it an injury. As if he was just hurt playing football. He was fucking shot..." Isabella mumbled to herself, still not believing the reality of it. "And I'm fucking preggers," she added, admitting to herself for the first time that she was pregnant, yet still not knowing what she was going to do or how she was going to tell her dad. Or Kian- for that matter. She is sick and she is scared. Well, guess it's just me and you for now, Kian Junior," she said as she gently rubbed her still-flat stomach and steeled herself to keep it a secret all the way to her delivery day rather than to see disappointment in her dad's loving eyes. Getting into her Kia Telluride, a birthday present from Kian when she turned 16 and got her drivers license, her car speakers began ringing, letting her know she had an incoming call through her phone's bluetooth, even though her phone is shut inside of her purse.

"Hello?" she said after accepting the call as she backed out of the driveway.

"Baby, listen, I can't make it tonight. I gotta handle something down in Miami," said Kian, sounding weird to Isabella.

"Kian, no! You said we could spend some time tonight and-"

"I know and I'm sorry, Sweetheart- something important came up and it can't wait-" started Kian, trying to excuse himself.

"So, I'm not important?"

"Huh? No! Baby, I mean yes, of course you're important. It's just that, well, they found my Auntie Nikki in Lil Haiti and I got-"

"Kian, no! Baby, no! Just let that shit go, baby. You can't keep-"

"Can't keep what? Let what go? My father's murder?"

"I'm not saying-"

"Look, Izzy, it's not a debate. I'm just letting you know I can't make it tonight. I'm sorry, baby. But this is something I've got to deal with myself and it's not something I can just let go. I've been waiting for two years for this call and-"

"I'm pregnant..." interrupted Isabella, causing a sudden silence after uttering those two words. She already regrets her big, fat mouth saying that without thinking first, but she made her bed and now she would have to lay in it. So would Kian, apparently. They were both tied together now by circumstances instead of love.

Chapter Six

Kilo

Kilo sat in the front passenger seat, Glizzy in the drivers, while Haze was in the back of the stolen Excursion, talking to his Lil Haiti contact, Smooth, a big and dark skinned pretty-boy type just trying to make his bones with Zoe Mafia Affiliates to get in on Haze's flaka connect, something he never shared with anyone outside their circle.

"I don't know, Haze. All I'm tryna tell you, is that yesterday, something had happened on 4th Court, and now today, she gone," said Smooth, cryptically.

"Did she know anything about you? About us?" asked Haze seriously.

"Are you for real, my nigga? Ain't no way!" answered Smooth. "Some jit got smacked yesterday, right over there," he pointed across the street towards a small cut in between buildings. "But I heard it was a bunch of jits, so probably no connection to her as far as I know..."

"And how long has she been living in Edison Projects?" asked Kilo, speaking for the first time since meeting Smooth.

"Shit, I been here a year and a half and she been here befo' me."

Kilo opened the door and got out of the big stolen truck. "Glizzy, you got some dope on you?" he asked, looking all around at all the fiends everywhere.

"Yea, why?"

"Gim'me a few lays," ordered Kilo, referring to crack that was called 'lays' in Palm Beach County- Lake Worth City mostly- not only their being flat like the Lays potato chip, but also because kids would buy Lays for $10 and 'parlay' them to the bassers for $20. Everywhere else, the crack is whipped so much that it blows up, looking a lot thicker, but only bubbles of air fill the space, a $20 will still weigh the same, even thought nobody actually weighs crack. The whole difference is that the whip just looks bigger or thicker, but Lake Worth bassers love Lays so they can see exactly what they were getting for their money, too experienced to fall for that 'water whip' game.

"What the..." started Glizzy, but instead of trying to guess at Kilo's tactics after knowing him for so many years and knowing that he does nothing without deep thought and heavy reasoning, he poured out his Garcia & Vega cigar vile and handed Kilo a few big flat pieces of crack rocks.

Kilo immediately walked down halfway into an alleyway where an old black, grey-haired smoker was sitting next to a shopping cart with only three working wheels, trying to drink his Steele Reserve 211 in peace. He approached him silently.

"Lem'me see your stem, Unc," said Kilo.

"Awl, nawl, jit! You's too young to be-" started the smoker.

"Cool out, old timer, I got something to put on ya pipe..." Kilo started, but before he even got the first five words out, the veteran smoker was handing him a glass rose stem, already sensing Kilo's reasoning and wanting this free high.

Kilo took a whole $20 and shoved it into the stem, all the way into the Char-Boy, Brillo-type of filter. Then, quickly handing it back to the anticipating hands of the 'buddy', who already had his lighter going as he swiftly shoved the other end of the rose stem into his almost white, crusty lips, as if afraid that Kilo would maybe change his mind and take back the free dope from him.

Kilo only smiled to himself being three years into the dope game, he was already desensitized to crack and the shit people do to obtain it, so he wasn't put out in the least when the smoker just looked at him, eyes bugging out of his head, not even saying thank you, or showing any gratefulness at all. It's all a part of the game.

"What's your name, Unk?"

"They call me 'Suga Ray' on account of I used to be his spar partner back in the 70's...and well, nephew, that was many years ago," he said, fidgeting a little bit from the crack blast.

"Okay, Suga Ray, you like that 110 octane gas I just put on the pipe for ya?"

"Sho' do! Damn right, nephew. Now what can ole Sug help you with?"

"That's the right answer, Unc. What I need is to know about that fight over there yesterday, you tell me about that, I got another blast for your rocket to take you right back to the moon..." offered Kilo, using his refined finesse game to open doors.

"Neph, I'll tell you, in all of my years of boxing, I ain't never be done seen such a damn mean-spirited and vicious monster as that Lil E. Just plain evil- an obnoxious lil devil- kicked the boy dead is what he did-"

"Who did?" asked Kilo, interrupting the old man's rant.

"Lil E, nephew! Ain't I said it already?" he answered, looking at Kilo quizzically. "You know, you favor that boy a lot in ya face, ya sho' y'all ain't no kin? Anyway, wasn't nothing but an after school fight that be done turned into a straight bloody murder, that's for sho. Saw all that shit, the boy can sho' fight, but one thing I know, you never hit below the belt and ya never kick a man when he down-"

"So, where they at now?"

"The police came, police left."

"So, this kid is Calico-Zoe's son?" Calico-Zoe made sho' wouldn't nobody tell the po-po anything about his evil son."

"Yea, something like that- hey, nephew, you sho' askin' a lot of quest-"

"Lem'me see ya stem, Unk," interrupted Kilo.

The smoker quickly forgot what he was about to say about his own observations, immediately handing over his rose stem to Kilo and watching closely as he stuffed another lay on his stem. His lighter was already fired up by the time Kilo was handing him his fully loaded stem back, and he didn't hesitate to devour the whole $20 rock in one big blast.

Eyes bugged out and obviously high as a kite, Sugar Ray was a very contented customer now. He looked up at Kilo expectantly, awaiting his purpose.

"So, Calico-Zoe's son- He beat the other kid to death. I got that. What about Calico- Zoe's girlfriend? Where's she at?" asked Kilo.

Sugar Ray then told him all of it..

Chapter Seven

Emelio

"But then what I'm finna do about school?" asked Emelio, still not sure that he is understanding what his mother is trying to say.

"Boy-bye with all of that shit! School ain't never helped nobody build no empire! Ya father ain't ever needed no school and he was really da man in these streets, fuck what Jeezy talkin' bout," answered Nikki, trying to school her son and get him ready to be the king of the streets and take off right where his father, Maniac, had left off at.

"I'm finna still go to school moms. I still wanna play football-"

"Boy! Kill all that football mess! You tryna play kids games? Or you finna get the bag and take yo daddy place on top?" she retorted, her aggravation apparent.

On and on it went, although Lil E knew that the outcome would always be the one that his mother had chosen for him, as it always was. Ever since he was old enough to understand words, he had been reminded who his father was and how he had some very big shoes to fill. It was always better to just acquiesce to her wants. Her demands. But not on this one. He wanted to keep playing football like he had it in his blood, and he had to go to school to play. Hence, their whole disagreement about going to school.

"A king needs his pawns, moms. You taught me that much. So, in order for me to build a team, I need to go to school to meet people. To build a rapport with my future constituents and all of that campaign trail shit-" started Lil E.

"Now you just making fun'na me! Fine, we gotta go to the 45th Street Flea Market anyway. We can get our new fake IDs and birth certificates done while we over there. Can't have you using ya real name after you bodied that boy in Edison PJs-"

"Or you bodied that girl at the hair salon."

"Boy-bye! Now you all up in my business! How you know bout that? I ain't 'body' that lil' dumbass girl! Probably should've though!" said Nikki with a smirk. "So, how did your meeting with Rosendo go? Did you make a good impression with your Spanish?"

"Yea, moms. I spoke Spanish to him, but you know he speaks English, so why I been all Rossetta Stone and shit? Plus, I'm getting my work from Jonjon and Calico-dem, and they speak Creole, so why learn a whole 'nother language for?"

"Because, Emelio, a king must always feed his soldiers. You never can have too many plugs, so you rotate your re-ups. One time you buy from Calico, then another time, Rosendo. Now, you've got two avenues, and you're keeping a secret on how much work you are really moving- letting them assume. They underestimate your value and don't know your real numbers."

"Why that matter, ma?"

"So, if a drought hits: One, you double your purchase number of units from the plug who still has, while showing your true hustling ability to both of them. Always keep shit close to your vest 'til it further benefits your position," said Nikki cryptically.

"What if they both run out?" questioned Lil E.

"*Now* you is thinkin' like a king. We also going to meet a backup plug today. You will be meeting PBSO evidence room officer Oscar Rojas. He is-"

"A fucking cop?" snapped Lil E. "I thought we don't talk to police?"

36

"Only when we payin' them to talk to us. But nah, Emelio. Think like a king again. Who is the only plug that gots dope when the whole South Florida is out?"

"I'm guessing that the PBSO evidence locker- is what you're telling me?" asked Lil E.

"Well, don't act all enthusiastic about it, I'm doing it all for-"

"For me?" asked Lil E, angrily interrupting. "Ma, whatever reason you doin' all this for, keep it a stack! You ain't done none of this fa me! Dis here? Dis fa you, ma, and you know it. On top of all that- ya done forgot that I don't even got the client base to support buying bricks yet..."

"Yea. About that: I been talkin' to Grey Goose and-" started Nikki.

"Ma! You be done brought Uncle Grey into this shit now?'

"Grey Goose knows the city and he knows the people. He can be of use. A rook, maybe. Plus, he's down-dick in the dirt- and he will be able to help you put shit together..."

Grey Goose was a well known hood legend among the kids as he had been a 'Kraze Barye' or Destroy the Barrier, before being a runner for the ex-Contra head Nicaraguan plug, 'Jit'. The DEA were still angry that they never were able to catch this Haitian who had been outsmarting them for years by driving loads of bricks hidden in auction wrecked vehicles that he was carrying on the flat bed of his Tic-Tac-Towing tow truck that he drives as a facade. He is also a Haitian Sensations member, although nobody really knew about it.

Grey was one who had beat the game. Suspected of several murders but he was never convicted of any of them. He got in, got his money and got out, simply put. He never wore jewelry or flossed in fancy cars. Every dime he got, he put into a car wash on 9th and Dixie Highway in Downtown Lake Worth. He had really made it.

Unfortunately for him, as his car wash began to lose money, all of Grey's investments had plummeted, Nikki had explained to Emelio, leaving him open to new opportunities. Emelio didn't like it. He knew and accepted that his mother was well versed in the dope game and street life, but he felt like she was not only pushing too hard, but going too damn fast as well. A sign of desperation. He doesn't agree with his mother about Grey. He thinks it's a bad move to bring him in. Use him for introductions and the like? Sure. But bringing in a Super Bowl MVP with 5 rings, 20 years after he's played his last game wasn't going to turn out the way she was thinking it would. Jits now-a-days were smarter, younger, and much thirstier. They would be running circles around Grey.

Emelio was definitely not feeling this move. It was a bad call, he thought. Kids these days are straight killers- it's a different world nowadays. Grey Goose wouldn't survive it long, unfortunately.

Chapter Eight

Kilo

Because all of them had left their phones in their respective cars back at the Lake Worth High School Tri-Rail station in an abundance of caution, being with all of the cell tower data and GPS OnStar tracking being exploited by police nowadays, they all missed calls from Isabella, Dice, Quan and Kilo's little brother Jermaine. But after having ditched the 'stolo' Excursion, they rode in the Tri-Rail's second floor train in silence before Kilo finally answered the question they were all already dying to know the answer to.

"Aunt Nikki has a son. A nigga named Lil E. So, Lil E just killed some kid, a bully I guess, in front of the whole Edison Projects, and Calico-Zoe pulled out his yopper and told everyone not to say shit or they'd be 'First 48'. Unc told me that right afterwards, Nikki flipped the script and packed up her and her son's shit and just split. He thinks they back in Palm Beach, but he can't know for sho, it's just rumers about Calico-Zoe heading our way.. ."

"I know that look on ya face, Lil Bruh. What's going on in that head of yours?" asks Glizzy, knowing Kilo too well not to notice his wheels turning.

"Well, I don't know exactly, ya know? When Unc was telling me all this, it didn't really register. I was looking at the bigger picture, but now..." Kilo said, trailing off.

"What, homie?" asked Haze, trying to prompt him to share whatever it is that was really bothering him, knowing Kilo didn't 'cry wolf' or raise false alarms.

"I don't know. I mean, this bitch been my so-called auntie for as long as I can remember her being in my life. Wouldn't I have been aware if this bitch had a kid? I mean he would somewhat be like my 'cousin' if she my 'auntie', so I'm lost on how this bitch all of the sudden got a kid my age, ya know? Something ain't right about it." Kilo said, trailing off.

"You think maybe momdukes knows and just never told you?" asked Glizzy.

"It's always possible, but somehow I really doubt it. It's just...man the shit just don't fit, it's like a puzzle piece, no matter how hard you tryna make it fit, it just ain't gon' fit cuz it don't go there. Whatever- it's probably nothing for reals, I just think it's weird, but I'ma talk wit' my ole girl when we get back to Lake Worth..."

"Nah, Lil Homie, it's definitely something. You've always had some really good instincts, so I would count on them being onto something too. I'll ask some more around and have Dice do the same before he leaves for Port Au Prince. I'm sure something will come up," said Haze, reassuring him.

Silence settled between them as they are the only passengers on the top deck of the double decker Tri-Rail train, speeding at more than 120 MPH towards Lake Worth High School's adjacent train station under the bridge.

Once back at their cars, parked in the high school parking lot, as opposed to the Tri-Rail lot located under the Interstate I-95 highway bridges, they all check their phones and begin returning calls as they drive away. Kilo doesn't even get a chance to call Isabella back before his phone starts ringing in his hand. He busts a right onto Lake Worth Road, heading East in his year old black Yukon on "28 Moonrockers, looking like the young boss that he was quickly becoming in the mean streets of Palm Beach County.

"Yeo," Kilo says answering his call on the Yukon's handsfree Bluetooth system, making anyone's conversation sound like talking to God with complete Memphis Audio sound system, pushing over 2,500 watts per "15 Memphis Mojo speaker.

"Bruh! Where the fuck you been at? Man, you seen our old girl?" asked Kilo's frantic little brother, Jermaine, obviously in distress over something.

"Nah, bruh, why you ask? What's going-"

"Man, Iceberg called and he seen her sneaking off behind the 12th Avenue store after that basser Nita had just copped some hard!"

"Shit, man. She was doing so-"

"That ain't all, Bruh! I'm just now finding out and Imani saying moms ain't been home in days and-" Jermaine says, trying to explain, but again Kilo interrupts him as he is just getting to his point.

"Why the fuck am I just now hearing about this shit, Jermaine? Shit, Bruh! She almost two years clean since she got shot by those fuckin' Y-Los in the drive-by at the crib," argued Kilo, praying this was some sort of a mistake.

"I know, man. It's royally fucked up. I mean she'd never leave Imani home alone at night! Ain't no way she'd leave her for two nights! Imani only 11 and all, shit... " Jermaine said, trailing off.

"Well, shit! Bruh, she been acting weird or anything lately?"

"Not that I seen, but I ain't been by over there since me and Jamie been staying at her place and shit..."

"You been *living* with Jamie?" asked Kilo heatedly.

"Yea, Bruh."

"Why the fuck ain't nobody telling me shit bout what's going on 'round here? Man, shit! Y'all keepin' secrets now?" Kilo demanded.

"Yea, cuz I be knowin' you gon' blow up bout it man, ain't no big deal, Bruh. Me and Jamie in love man-" started Jermaine.

"In love?!" Kilo screamed, interrupting Jermaine. "Man, you 14 years old! And she 20! Bruh, calm ya lil ass down with all that 'love' shit, Bruh..."

"See? And that's the shit I be talkin' bout, right there. A nigga don't tell you shit cuz you overreact and shit-"

"My bad, Bruh. Look, I'm on "A" Street. I'll be there in a second, so meet me there," said Kilo, as he disconnected the call and turned onto 12th Avenue South. Southside L- Dub. The hood. His Hood.

Chapter Nine

Isabella

Isabella had a very bad day. After having found out that she was pregnant, she was having a little spat with Kian over his missing their date tonight and skipping the most important tests of the school year in order to go to Miami and try to exact a razor's edge of revenge on a bitch who had been having no parts of their lives in the last two years or more. So, she had just spit it out. Right in the middle of their damn argument! She couldn't believe that she had been so damn foolish and careless. Why had she done that?! No wonder he had reacted in the way that he had. She had just dumped this on him as he wasn't already going through enough and overly stressed out. "I'm pregnant..." she had said on the phone.

His reaction? Fucking silence! Crickets chirping and shit with no comment forthcoming. That was her fault though, wasn't it? she wondered. I mean, if I had sat him down in a neutral and relaxed environment, then felt him out with children related questions *before* telling him the news, his reaction would've been way different. It could've allowed him to have a lot more of a positive reception, wouldn't it? she wondered. Maybe. But then again, maybe not. Maybe he wasn't ready, she thought to herself, playing the Devil's advocate. Shit, like I am? Maybe he is scared...Shit, and I'm not? she asked herself. The main point is that he hadn't considered *her* fears or *her* feelings. How was his reaction supposed to make *her* feel? she wondered further to herself.

Well, either way, even though- to her- that had been her *most* traumatic experience of the day, it hadn't been her *only* traumatic experience of the day. That was for sure.

She had been in P.E. after exams, which were done when they were still fresh in the morning, and while she had been at her team's volleyball practice, she had been hit in the face with a spiked ball and had apparently fainted. She was woken up in the emergency room at JFK Hospital. Her father's hospital.

Great, she thought to herself, waking up and now my dad has to find out I'm pregnant at 16 with all of his colleagues here in the middle of my business. Shit, he is literally going to kill me. I can't even imagine what he's going to do to Kian! Oh, shit! Kian!

Now a realistic fear is coming across her chest. She can't bare to have been responsible for disappointing her father, but that's exactly what was going to happen if they were to take her bloodwork. She knows for a fact that they do those tests automatically upon admission to the hospital, so she was going to have to hope and pray that nobody has the heart to tell her dad. She would beg and plead if need be, even go as far as throwing herself on the mercy of the court-or physician this instance.

"Well, Izzy, your vitals are back to normal and we've got you on a saline solution IV drip to dilute the nutrients we are going to give you and to help hydrate your body. It's only dehydration that caused you to fall out, not a good thing for a healthy pregnancy to..." started the doctor, before Isabella desperately interrupted her.

"Please don't tell my dad, Dr. Bezares! I would-"

"Sweetheart, I'm sorry," said Dr. Carmen Bezares, interrupting Isabella right back. "He's the one who brought me the bloodwork tests and asked for the prenatal nutrients to be added to your IV to help regulate your health for the baby's sake."

Isabella had never been so speechless and scared in her life.

44

"I will tell you this, though, honey," said the Puerto Rican Doctor Bezares. "You need to have a serious talk with your father. You should know better, Izzy."

"I know, I should have been using protection-" started Isabella.

"I'm not talking about that, Izzy. I'm talking about you should know better about how your father feels about you! That man adores you! He's not mad at you for being 16 and pregnant, Sweetie. He's upset that you felt you couldn't trust him to talk to him about it and come to him for help...*That* really hurt him. Now, after you've talked and worked it out, you let me know what you plan to do and-"

"Plan to do?" asked Isabella, interrupting again.

"About your pregnancy..."

"I'm going to have my baby. I don't believe in abortion..."

"Very well then," said Dr. Bezares, writing something in her chart about her decision and scheduling a future prenatal appointment.

Now, being left to her own devices, she had to gather up the courage to talk to her father and to think of what she could actually say to him to keep him from killing Kian. It will be a tall order, but she knows her father better than anyone in the world, and she knows he will understand her love for Kian. After all, they've been together for over two years now, ever since he purposely 'accidentally' bumped into her in the cafeteria getting their lunch on the first day of school, using that lame technique to get her attention and start up a conversation with her. Even though it was a little lame, she thought the effort was cute, so she had let him in, and the last two years had been her best time ever. Until now, that is.

She stopped stressing for a minute, smiling at Kian's lame attempt to get her attention and about the love they share. Suddenly, her confidence was back. They loved each other more than anything and they would work it out. After all they had faced together and all they'd been through, they would work through it- like they always have. She smiled again. They would work it out. She knew they would. They would have to, because now, it wasn't about just them.

Finally, in walked Kian, a worried and stressful look deeply etched into his features on his handsome face. Jermaine followed behind him, smiling to her with his unspoken support, a good reason why she really loved them both: Their loyalty and dedication.

Chapter Ten

Kilo

The assailant waited behind the black Cadillac Escalade with big, shiny rims on it. He was pretty sure that this was his target's truck. He isn't good with makes and models of vehicles. He is not that type of man. He just knows that his target drives a big, black truck with big and shiny wheels.

The assailant's target comes into the parking lot, away from the bright lights. The assailant begins to panic as he realizes that his target is veering left from his current position. He isn't coming to his truck, he is going to the North side of the parking lot for some reason. Why? he asks himself.

But then, the assailant sees it, further off: Another big, black truck on big wheels. Shit, thinks the assailant, his truck is way over there!

The assailant is an avid jogger and a health nut in the best shape of his life, so it takes him no longer than half a minute to make it three cars down in the same row as his target hits the unlock button on his key fob and approaches the driver's side door.

The assailant sprints the last few paces, quickly covering ground as he is simultaneously drawing out his .380 Taurus and then he racks the slide, chambering a round, but also alerting his target to his presence in the row of cars. The target had just been reaching for the door handle of his beloved GMC Yukon when he heard the tell-tale sound of a round being chambered into a semi-automatic, small caliber handgun. He turned quickly, reaching for his own .40 caliber Glock yet stopped himself just as suddenly, seeing his murderer's handgun already up and trained right between his eyes, simply waiting on the right provocation to fire his small, silver gun. It was over. Kilo didn't have a chance. The assailant straight up had the drops on him.

Seeing the target raising his hands ever so slowly, the assailant himself hesitates, not so sure about this after all. He has thousands of things running through his mind. He suddenly isn't so sure he can kill another human being. Actually take a life in cold blood.

He begins to let the weight of the gun slowly being his hand lower, millimeter by millimeter, one inch, then two. Then, all in an instant, in that split second of time, his target's face began to hint at recognition. It started in his target's eyes, but quickly spread to the rest of his face. His target recognizes him.

POP! POP! POP!

The target went backwards, slamming against the door of his big black truck, breaking the drivers side window, either from the bullets themselves, that had passed through the target's chest and shoulder just under the collar bone in two places, yet not too far from his heart either.

The assailant panicked again, dropping his gun and turning to run away and flee from the reality of the act that he had just committed and the possible ramifications for committing those actions and what a future for a shooting assailant might be. He ran and got all the way to the other side of the parking lot before remembering that his car was parked in the middle lot. Right on front street. He took off the Covid mask, which was really just a medical mask to prevent the spreading of germs to patients, and he slowed his walk to make it as casual as he could. It was too late for caution though, he had dropped the gun at the scene of the crime. A gun that was registered to him. In his name.

For God's sake, what was I thinking? he asked himself rhetorically. It was rhetorical because he knew exactly what he was thinking, as would everyone when they found out who the victim was, and who the gun was registered to.

Chapter Eleven

Emelio

A few weeks had passed since Lil E had put his foot down about attending Lake Worth High School and joining the football team. It was exciting to him. All the other hood shit and money making he was doing after school for his mother was cool too, he could not really complain about it, yet he felt forced and his heart wasn't really into it. Not like it was with football.

With football, he felt like he was really meant for it- was born to play. But, with the street shit, he was only doing it to please his mother, well, excluding the fighting. He loved fighting. It being a kind of sport. Lil E loves all sports, so of course he would enjoy fighting. He had already been in a couple of fights around 12th Avenue South by "C" Terrace. The bigger kid, a bully of sorts he had knocked out with a nasty left hook, breaking his glass jaw.

But when he had fought this other smaller kid, he had been surprised by not only his heart, but the fact that he had no *quit* in him whatsoever. He had been even more impressed when, a few days later, he approached the kid at 12th Avenue corner store and he had immediately balled his fists and started to put up his set. He recalled the event.

"Whoa-whoa-whoa, homie. I ain't lookin' fa no smoke. I was just finna handle up and wanted to squash shit when I seen ya..." said Lil E.

"Why?" asked the tough-looking kid who looked to be around the same age as Lil E. "Don't nobody squash no beef 'round here unless it benefits them. So, what you want?"

Lil E chuckled a little bit at that because it's the same thing he would be thinking if he was in this kid's position. Being raised around Edison Projects in Lil Haiti trained you at a young age to suspect everyone's motives- even your own mother- and to remain cynical. Lil E can really relate to this kid, like two different sides on a fresh Blue Face, they were the same at the end of the day, and that is something truly hard to find in this environment.

"From you? Nothing. But from your city? I want everything," Lil E answered, being entirely too cryptic for the young kid he was.

The kid before him only responded with a dubious look, still guarded; and not knowing how to respond to such a weird statement. Such a awkward situation. He isn't sure if Lil E is playing games with him or not, so he doesn't comment. It's still an unorthodox situation that he's found himself in, after only fighting this other kid days ago.

"Ayo, homie. I ain't on nothing, bruh. I just moved up here from Lil Haiti in Miami and I'ont know nobody and shit...so, my bad bout before, bruh. I'm new, I'ont know who's who, ya feel me? But I respect ya heart, bruh. You thuggin' fa real..." said Lil E in his own lil attempt of a halfway apology, overlooking the fact that this kid had bumped into him at the corner store and started the whole thing. But one thing he said that he knew was real talk, was that he definitely respected the other kid's heart. And his hands. This kid can fight.

"Oh," he answered, taken off guard for a moment. "Aww, bruh. It's all good. Ain't no harm done. I know how it is when you new. I moved to the Southside of L-Dub and been squabbling ever since then," he smiled. An opening in his tough exterior.

"Yea, I guess it always sucks being the new kid. What's ya name, homie?" asked Emelio as he fires up the half blunt of his special blend of exotics that he had in his ear from earlier. He took a deep draw of the potent weed smoke and offered it over to his new found friend.

"I'm Jermaine, but er'body calls me Jay. What's yours?" Jay asked before taking the blunt and hitting it, causing him to cough a couple times.

"Take it easy, bruh. That's gas right there...I'm Emelio, but I go by Lil E..." he stated and then took the remainder of the blunt back with a chuckle.

"Damn! Tha-that's-that shit fye, bruh..." said Jay, stuttering and trying to find his equilibrium back after being hit so hard from the potent concentrated dose of THC.

Emelio could do nothing but laugh. He actually was having a good time just being able to kick it like a normal teen and smoke a blunt with another kid. He was always training or learning the game when around Calico-Zoe and all his Zoe Pound homies, always having a hard stare-gangsta facade on, he forgot what it was like to be a kid. It felt kind of good to him.

"Yea, bruh, it's definitely some fye. I got this shit for days if you know who tryna cop...shit, I got it where you can middleman this shit and make a few dollars if you want to. Looks like you be knowin' a lot of girls that smoke," said Lil E, shifting his eyes toward Jamie, who was waiting in the truck on Jay.

"Yea, bruh. I do. All my girl's friends be lookin' fa some gas like that and da shit I been havin' be pretty damn good, but it ain't like *that*...what *is* that shit anyway? That shit got me high like da moon!" said Jermaine with his eyes halfway closed off of a couple hits that he had taken off of the blunt.

"That there is mostly Cereal Milk. But I mixed in some White Runtz for flavors and sprinkled some moon rock in for a good kick. I'm kind of like a THC poet, or a weed mixologist. I make it how I personally like it. Mixing is the newest form of exotic. You ain't gotta crossbreed strains anymore to make some gas. Gorilla Glue and Girl Scout Cookies ain't really shit to me no mo'. Plus that moon rock really takin' off now, mostly in Miami, but I bet it could take off in Palm Beach too..." said Lil E, trailing off as he began to contemplate an idea in his head. "Say, bruh. Would you be able to push it to da limit like Ross if I can get it to ya?"

Chapter Twelve

Kilo

After being shot three times in his chest, he was incredulous. Kilo is a gangsta and had been shot before, so it wasn't being shot that really has him going into shock. It was that he had figured out who the shooter was, despite the baby blue Corona mask that he had been wearing, covering most of his face. It wasn't even that hard to figure. It's all in the eyes. Nobody but the one closest to him has those eyes. Eyes that he would never- *could* never- forget.

He has no valid understanding of why he wasn't completely panicking or freaking out right now, only assuming that since he doesn't really feel too much pain, it must not be that bad. Mostly he just felt numb. The sound in his ears was a ringing that almost blocked out his hearing. After the first shot, he didn't even hear the rest, so in his mind, he only had thought he was hit once.

This shooting is a complication that he doesn't need. Not right now with all that is going on, especially with the person that actually shot him. That's definitely some smoke he don't want. Nope. Not at all.

Trying to stay calm, one hand on his chest, trying to stop the bleeding, he grabs his iPhone from his white Chrome Hearts shorts. Well, shorts that *used* to be white, since they are now soaking up all of the blood running from his bullet hole. Holes? he noticed for the first time. He had more than one hole. He had three.

Dialing on his phone, he quickly called Jermaine's number, knowing he was still inside of the hospital. 911 is not even in his vocabulary, so he never even contemplated that as a viable option.

"Hey, Key. Did you forget-" started Jermaine after answering on the second ring, knowing it was his brother by his YNW Melly ring tone.

"Jay!" yelled Kilo, not really hearing Jermaine too well. "I need you to come to my truck ASAP! I got shot! Bring some doctors and shit man, I'm bleedin' pretty bad-"

"I'm on my way," said Jermaine, barely audible to Kilo, trying to remain calm, yet struggling. "Man who shot ya, Bruh?!"

"Listen, Bruh! Listen carefully..." he paused as he could barely hear Jermaine talking to someone else, medical staff most likely, inside the lobby of JFK, trying to get him some medical help.

"Bruh, we on our way now! Stay strong, Bruh! Just hold-" started Jermaine, once he came back on the phone before Kilo interrupted him again.

"Listen to me carefully, Jay! I'm hiding the guns in the inside of the front wheel of the white Honda parked next to my truck! Make sure you take them and hide them! Don't let-"

"I see your truck, bruh! I heard ya too! Just hang on! I'm comin'!"

After securing both of the guns, leaving his own inside of its specially fitted paddle holster, while waiting for medical help, he sat contemplating all that was going wrong in his life all of a sudden: His mother missing; Aunt Nikki getting away; his brother having moved out of his mom's house at 14 and in with some white chick too old for him; and now he has been shot three fucking times in his chest. He's definitely not having a good day, week, or month.

As he is thinking about all of this, he flashes back to the face of the man that shot him. Those eyes. Unmistakable eyes. It's always in the eyes. He is not wrong, he knows who shot him and he definitely knew why. He would definitely be taking both of those details to his grave. He can never let anyone know about this. His shooter was far too important to allow his homies to retaliate against him.

Those were his last thoughts before he finally passed out, succumbing to the pain and blood loss. Having lost so much blood at this point, his consciousness eluded him. Some paramedics who had just dropped off somebody who was injured in a car accident, just happened to be there and available to provide a quick response to Kilo's plight and ran behind Jermaine with a gurney to get him into the emergency room and onto an operating table as quickly as possible. They all knew that timing is everything when dealing with GSWs, or gun shot wounds, the faster they get on the operating table and get treated, the better the chances are for survival.

§§§§

Once Jermaine had gotten his big brother the help he needed, he didn't immediately follow the EMS people back inside the JFK emergency room. He knew he had something to do for his big brother first. Being that police were always notified as a routine procedure at Florida hospitals upon arrival of any victims of GSWs, Jermaine knew his time was limited before the cops' arrival.

Trying to look natural, yet looking around the parking lot to make sure it was clear, Jermaine ducked down next to the front passenger wheel of the Honda backed-in next to his brother's GMC Yukon. Reaching behind the wheel, he pulled out his brother's- what used to be his father's- Glock, which was in a paddle holster and clipped it onto his belt. Then he reached and grabbed the other gun, a silver .380 with bloody finger prints smudged all over it. His brother's blood apparently.

He quickly slipped it into his back pocket as he stood up, starting to make his way back to the JFK hospital entrance. As he was walking back, he called his mother's phone first. It went straight to voicemail. Shaking his head, he hit his big brother's day-one nigga, Quan. He knew it as facts, that they would immediately want to retaliate, being that Kilo was a high ranking member in good standing with the infamously violent Zoe Mafia Affiliates family, an organization known for its violence on ops.

Because Jermaine hadn't ever met or been around the ZMA or his brother's big homies, he couldn't call them directly, hence the necessity of involving Quan, his brother's best friend and day one nigga.

"What's good, Jay?" asked Quan, answering the call, but knowing something was up for Jermaine to be calling him instead of Kilo. "Bruh been shot! We at JFK! He wouldn't tell me who did it, but I got both guns and-" started Jermaine, somewhat scared for his brother's life and talking too fast.

"Okay, okay, Lil Bruh. Just calm down. I'm sho he finna be a'ight, this ain't his first rodeo. I'm on my way now. Don't talk to nobody, bruh. Especially them damn pigs, so if they try to talk-"

"That's a big duh, bruh! I wouldn't never talk to them."

"A'ight, bruh. Facts. I'm on my way..." said Quan, hanging up on Jermaine so he could get there faster and before he said anything else unnecessary on a phone line, not knowing who might be listening and knowing dirty police tactics like everyone else not putting anything past them.

Chapter Thirteen

Nikki

It wasn't unusual for bums and bassers to be sitting out in front of the mini-plaza on 12th Avenue South, where there was a phone store for Metro PCS and T-Mobile; an Arab store; and a very popular beauty salon called Murdle's. There were always so many kinds of different people frequenting and loitering in front of the store, hustlers; bassers; and bums alike, so it wasn't an unusual sight that Nikki saw when she pulled up at 7pm to her late hair and nail appointment with Murdle. She simply parked her Genesis GV70, got out and entered the store to get a health shake to drink on before hand, having just left the gym, so she could drink it, replenishing her electrolytes while getting her hair done.

As Nikki approached the door to the Arab store, the rest of her surroundings were like background noise to her. Her life was starting to look up, as her plan toward taking over the 561 were seeming to come to fruition and soon, she knew that her son would be taking the reigns and running shit. So she was generally in a good mood, and was distracted by those ambitious thoughts on her mind when she entered the Arab store, missing the bum sitting up against the wall, blending in, right in front of the phone store.

Nikki went to the counter and payed after selecting her favorite shake and moved towards the door in preparation to exit the store and go over to her hair appointment. She is only thinking about her future plans and her immediate need to get her nails and hair done, so she is completely oblivious to her dangerous surroundings. Her mind thinking at 100 MPH caused her to completely miss the fact that the basser in the black hoodie had moved his spot from near the front door of the phone store, to the opposite side, in between the Arab store and the beauty salon, a thing that wouldn't have caught her attention anyway, since most people see these bums and bassers as telephone poles or furniture. Something easily overlooked, never taking notice of them.

It was absolutely this particular basser's intention to be overlooked and to stay seen as background. This particular basser had heard through the Lake Worth Grapevine that the target, Nicole Lewis, was back in town and in action. Available to be seen and taken care of, in fact.

From Grey Goose came an explanation to some local hood figures as to his intentions of getting back into the game. That filtered down to some of the bassers, one of whom was Nita, a friend of Skyla, who immediately poured her a drink about these rumor updates, loving the gossip. Skyla was elated. She had went further into a hood investigation and finally gotten a connect at the beauty shop on 12th through Nita's people and got lucky to get Nikki's appointment from there.

Skyla had been keeping Nita on her team and in turn, Nita had helped to set up their whole scene today. So far, things had been going perfectly, just as planned.

Nikki was oblivious to all that was going on around her and that made things that much easier for the plot on her life to be accomplished successfully. Pushing through the door, she exited the Arab store. Nikki twisted off the cap of the drink mix as she took a few steps away from the door to allow other patrons to enter into the store.

The bum in the black hoodie was laying on the walkway, a cup for change in front of him. He started to stand up, and this too escaped Nikki's attention, her concentration all on opening her drink bottle.

In a split second and a flash of movement, it was all over and the health drink lie on the floor, spilling its contents out on the walkway and co-mingling with another, even darker substance: Nicole Lewis' life-blood.

Chapter Fourteen

Detective Jones

Detective Jones had received the call about a homicide on 12th Avenue South, an area very well known for its many homicides as well as drug sales and gang activity, so he already was expecting the worst. He wasn't let down when he got there either.

At first, he was surprised to see that he actually knew and had dealt with the victim before when she had been the victim of an attempted murder case that he had caught a few years ago. When the Mercedes she had been a passenger in had been shot 11 times, causing them to crash into other parked cars, he had been called in on the scene. But he quickly put his personal feelings aside and put his first responsibility at the top of his priorities list. He had to investigate the crime and ultimately find the killer.

First, he went looking for one of his trusty pocket notebooks, looking for the one in his glove box from a few years ago, since he went through about two or three of those notebooks a year. Once he had found the one he was looking for and found the right page, he flipped some more around the surrounding pages in it, putting together all of the events that had transpired during that time period and what connection it all might have had with his victim here today.

Looking at the notes he had made about the shooting of the brand new Mercedes S550 only four blocks from here, he saw that he had questioned Nicole Lewis but that the driver of the vehicle, Sintero Rodriguez, he later found out his name to be, had ultimately been uncooperative with him. They had apparently just dropped off a Skyla Hayworth and-

Yes, now it was all coming back to him. Skyla Hayworth's husband had been murdered at that same "C" Terrace address and he had never been able to solve that case. The address was just up the street. Maybe he would drop by over there and check on Skyla Hayworth. He remembered another shooting too, a drive-by, that had happened at that same address, deep in ZMA territory. He thought back, trying to recall, and it hit him: Skyla Hayworth had been struck in the arm by one of the stray bullets, assuming she wasn't the actual target of the shooting herself, which was highly unlikely, as he recalled her appearance after having dealt with her as well as her attitude and character.

Now that he thought about it, there were four shootings that seemed to be connected to Skyla Hayworth, who was a friend of Nicole Lewis, his newest victim. One, was her murdered husband; two, Nicole Lewis and Sintero Rodriguez's Mercedes; three, the drive-by shooting at her house where she was hit; and then, Jones thought back to the massacre in a Delray Beach mechanic shop, Grove Custom Auto, and the numerous bodies left behind in the worst blood bath of Delray Beach's history, and Sintero Rodriguez's mutilated and tortured body, left in a mess of blood, brains, and a pureed mush of body parts all blown off here and there. Number four. Four is just too many.

This was just too much to be a coincidence. Maybe one or two, but four different incidences? All some way or another connected, and Skyla Hayworth was in the middle of it all. Yes, he thought to himself, I'm definitely going to have to go and have a little chat with Mrs. Hayworth for sure.

§§§§

An hour later, Detective Jones sat at a PBSO computer in his unmarked cruiser, watching the surveillance footage as he was investigating the robbery and murder of this victim that he had known personally, and actually had a crush on last time they met.

As he viewed the footage, he-like Nikki-hadn't payed any attention to the bum in the black hoodie as he sat down on the walkway begging for change. But his focus came immediately back to him as he jumped up while his victim had tipped her head back to drink from the bottle she had just bought from the store.

It happened in a split second...

It had happened so fast that Jones had needed to restart it and watch it frame by frame, to actually see the whole effect of the assailant's move. He saw it frame by frame. There was less than a hundred frames of photographic evidence showing the actual murder. First, as the victim tipped her bottle up, she fully exposed her throat, leaving it open and unguarded, ripe for a strike against it.

In the next few frames, this is exactly what Jones watched happen. He saw that the assailant in fact wasn't a bum, and those big glasses that the blind seem to favor were a prop, as this assailant was obviously not blind.

In the frames, the bottle tipped upward, the throat was exposed, while simultaneously, the hooded figure jumped up almost like an athlete and flicked something in his hand. Jones froze the frame and hit the magnify icon, selecting the area to zoom in on with his thumb and index fingers on the touchscreen and enlarged the assailant's hand.

Taking his time and messing with the options, he was able to make out that the object in the assailant's hand was in fact a box cutter, which made perfect sense and jibed with the condition in which he had found the body in.

He turned back to the frame by frame viewing option and watched in horror as the vic again tipped the bottle up. The assailant jumped. He flashed the box cutter in a quick movement, slashed at the victim's throat while it was exposed, then pushed her to the ground and began to rifle through her clothes, conducting a search of her pockets, all while her life-blood was wasting on the dirty floor. He took some rings off of her fingers, popped her necklace, grabbed her purse and ran to a midsize black SUV, taking off in the luxury truck with some obviously expensive rims on it. It *could* be a normal robbery, mused Jones to himself. Yet, that is not what his gut was telling him, and 90% of detective work was based off of the gut of that detective. He needed to find out more and fast.

While he had been waiting for the store owner, a kindly Arab fellow, to copy his camera's footage from the cloud to a thumb drive for him, he thought back to when he had just stopped by Skyla Hayworth's residence on "C" Terrace, where a pre-teen girl had said that her mother hadn't been home at that time and didn't know when she might be back home. So, that had been a bust, but not for long, he thought.

He had canvassed the area, but who was he kidding? Didn't nobody know nothin', ain't seen or heard nothin', just how Trick Daddy's song said it would be. This is the Southside of Lake Worth, with more murders on this block than all of the other cities in Palm Beach County put together. They obviously weren't going to just start talking now all of a sudden. He knows that he has his work cut out for him. But this is what he does. This is his life and his reality, so he will make his arrest, just as he usually did.

Chapter Fifteen

Kilo

He woke up with his whole body feeling as if it had been run over by a Mack truck. He was completely immersed in pain while trying to not only remember what happened, but also to remember his name as well as who he actually was.

Opening his eyes was a task all in itself, but once he accomplished it, he took in his surroundings tentatively. He heard the beep-beep of the heart monitor and saw the IV drip that was attached to his arm. He began to panic, the beep-beep of the monitor beginning to speed up. He couldn't remember what happened, couldn't see why he was in this hospital bed at all. What had happened to him? he wondered to himself.

A face popped up and into his line of sight. Jermaine. He remembers now. His little brother. And now he knows that he is Kian, also known as Kilo in the streets, a nickname that his dad-Maniac, had given him as a boy. They were all members of the ZMA, or the Zoe Mafia Affiliates organization and were really getting to the bag in Palm Beach County.

His position holds rank in his set. "He's awake! He's awake!" said Jermaine, excitedly looking all around and Kilo realizes that there are other people inside of the hospital room with him.

Suddenly, a beautiful yellow girl's face pops up into his view with a huge smile on her pretty face. Kilo unintentionally and unknowingly jumps. It was her eyes. Her eyes, for some strange reason scared him into flinching and he had no idea why this was. Jermaine and the girl exchanged an uncomprehending and questioning look between them. Kilo tries to talk then.

"Wh-wha happon' to me?" Kilo asked, barely intelligible and wondering if he was in an accident.

"Hey, hey, bruh...Don't try to talk, okay?" said Jermaine before looking over at the beautiful girl. "Hey, Isabella, why don't you go get a nurse and let them know he's awake, okay?"

She worriedly looked at Kilo, confusion etched into her brow, but she nods in agreement, then leans over to kiss Kilo on his forehead, and this time, he doesn't flinch, as he now knows that she is Isabella, his girlfriend of almost three years now.

"Are you okay, bruh?" asked Jermaine with a concerned look on his face.

"Yea, I think so...I-I, what happened, bruh?" asked Kilo.

"Fool, you don't remember anything, bruh?"

"Nah, Jay. Talk to me..." said Kilo, still waking up and trying to gather his wits about himself.

"Well, you had called me from the parking lot at JFK sayin' that a nigga be done shot ya! Then you wouldn't answer me bout who did it. All you told me was to get the guns that you had hidden in the wheel of a car next to your truck. So, I went and got you help, then when nobody was around, I grabbed the guns..."

"Fuck, Jay! I can only remember bits and pieces, but I don't get why I would have another gun besides mines, unless I somehow .. I somehow took it from the shooter...I just don't know, shit," said Kilo, the confusion evident on his facial features.

At that moment, a nurse stepped in with Isabella on her heels, not going to miss any update about his status and recovery.

"And how are we feeling, Mr. Hayworth?" asked a slim and pretty ebony-skinned nurse as she was checking numbers on his attached machines and writing down the results on the clip board that had been in a slot on his hospital bed.

"How I'm 'sposed to know? Ain't you 'sposed to tell *me* how I'm is?" Kilo retorted with am attitude evident in his speech pattern and facial expressions.

"C'mon, baby. She's just doing her job and checkin' on you..." said Isabella, trying to do her best to mediate things because she knew most of the staff at the hospital her father works at and wants them to like her boyfriend as she does.

"And that's okay, Izzy. He's just going through a traumatic experience and is scared. It's quite normal actually, he's-" started the nurse again.

"First off, ain't nobody *scared* of shit! This ain't my first time on either side of that fire and I'm sho' it ain't finna be the last..." said Kilo, his aggravation and stress pretty evident for all present to see.

"Okay. Well, if it's not gonna be your last, I would definitely recommend investing in a Kevlar vest, because one or two inches lower and you wouldn't be here to give us your slick and clever comments. You would be dead and the child in Izzy's belly would be another fatherless child. Is that what you want? Well, is it, tough guy? Think on it-or next time don't ask for our help, okay?" said the nurse, replacing the clipboard in its slot on the the bed and walking toward the door, full of angry indignation.

"Was that really necessary, Kian?" asked Isabella, visibly shaken by the comments.

"Gim'me outta here, fuck all that shit she talkin' bout. C'mon, Jermaine, help me up..." said Kilo, pushing himself up before collapsing in pain back down onto the bed.

"Hey, bruh. Just relax okay? Fool, you can't leave yet..."

"Fuck..." said Kilo, resigned that he couldn't leave. He just sat back and looked as pissed off as he could, until he finally passed back out.

Chapter Sixteen

Emelio

It had only been a week that Lil E had been fronting not only the moon rock, as he had promised Jay, but also some of his own special blend of a exotic that nobody in the 561 could compete with, and he was amazed. Jay hadn't been lying about his ability to move the product with all of his girl's college friends at FAU in Boca Raton. He had been hard at work and it showed by his numbers.

Lil E had also been bossing up on his cocaine and heroin movements through Grey Goose, mostly selling cocaine in crack form around the neighborhood between 5th Avenue South and 4th Avenue North, leaving that already ZMA claimed 6th Avenue South all the way to 18th Avenue South alone. For now, that is.

He was cool with moving his mother's work with his mother's connections and all that.

It was all profit, but he never felt like it was his. He hadn't built these connections with these plugs. Or these hustlers. All these workers now on his team had been all of Grey Goose's homies and contacts. Again, Lil E couldn't complain, but it still wasn't his movement.

With the moon rocks and exotic, it was *all* his move. He had orchestrated it all without the help of his mother. While going to Miami Edison Senior High, he had been going with a beautiful tan and skinny Jamaican girl named Tasha. She had introduced him to her Uncle Granville, the top shotta to the Miami Jamaicans, and now, his own plug for the imported moon rocks and the exotic kush he was now flush with. He had also met his new lil homie,

Jay, on his own as well. So, the THC market was all his own lane, his influence and moves, all by himself.

Feeling accomplished in his own right, he was now cruising the streets with his recently purchased 2024 black Ford Maverick, a small body truck, only light tints on the windows and no shoes on the feet. His point was to have a vehicle to move around in without drawing any unwanted attention or causing himself to get pulled over, as the fake ID from the 45th Street Flea market would most likely not pass inspection if ran by the police. So, staying low-key had been his goal in purchasing this small work truck, and it definitely accomplished that.

So far this week, Jay had hit him up for more work twice a day until yesterday. Lil E had issued him two ounces of moon rock and a pound of his special blend of potent zaza this time, so it should last him at least a week, but with the way that Jay had been surpassing his expectations, he wouldn't be surprised if he didn't even make it a week with all of that work. FAU was the deciding factor for Emelio. This kid was singlehandedly bringing him a whole fucking college campus. He knew from watching *How High 2* with DC Young Fly, that once word got around at Florida Atlantic University, AKA "Find Another University", that they had that exclusive zaza, as well as moon rock, they would take over the game. He could then begin introducing his cocaine and heroin, but he was missing key elements. Flaka and molly.

Miami had every drug known to man, and at prices so low that nowhere but Texas could compare with its prices. But one thing that Zoe Pound *didn't* have in Miami, was a good flaka connect. But in Palm Beach County, the Zoe Mafia Affiliates and Haitian Sensations had the flaka on lock. Their connect was so good that Zoe Pound had even reached out to them through Haitian Sensations, trying to use their connect so they could undercut the Cubans in Hialeah on the flaka. So far, politics hadn't worked. ZMA wouldn't give up the connect, although they were amenable to middleman the work. All for a small fee of course.

This is where Lil E felt like he could really shine. If he could find a flaka connect on his own, without Grey Goose or his mother's help or contacts, he would have found another avenue to make his own way in the game. It would be his hustle alone. Just like his moon rocks and exotic hustle. He had skill in seeing potential in something to turn a profit with. That is his gift. It is also his advantage over his mother, Calico-Zoe, Grey Goose, and anyone their age. They are all old school. Lil E is from the new school. Cocaine and heroin, or dirt weed? Are they serious? his reaction had been when dealing with his mother and her generation of hustlers and friends. They didn't see the profit margin in moon rocks and exotics. They laughed about his ideas of molly and flaka, calling them 'designer drugs' and 'synthetic shit'.

"What we really need to move into, is meth," his uncle Grey Goose had said at one point, not even trying to hear Lil E's objections, treating him like a lil nigga. He tried to explain that the Mexican Matamoros Cartel had pretty much split the monopoly on the meth trade with the Sinaloa Cartel and they, as Haitians, had no way around the way the cartels mass produced that shit, making it impossible to compete with their low prices on weight.

Basically, Lil E saw the future with these new drugs, and his mother and her people only saw old people's drugs as money makers. It was because they knew about those old drugs. They had learned about those drugs and gotten complacent. But Lil E wouldn't give up, there is a lot of money in these new school drugs, he would just have to *show* his mother and Uncle Grey. They would have to see it to believe it. But they had once needed to see to believe what a difference just adding baking soda to some coke in boiling water would make. And that was a combination that had changed the world in the 80's. What would he be able to do? he wondered to himself. Two words came to mind: Take Over.

He decided to call his mother since he hadn't heard from her since he had left his football practice, which was definitely unusual in the sense that she was usually checking on him by now, trying to make sure that he was on his grind, so to speak. His first call went unanswered. That was definitely weird. Maybe she was on the phone with Calico-Zoe on the other line, he surmised. He tried again, but the answering party was not his mother, and the news he received was not good at all. It was actually the worst news he had ever received in his life since Lemonhead had left them to go on the run from the authorities.

"Hello?" asked the deep baritone of an authoritative voice. "Who the fuck is this?" Lil E asked with an attitude, knowing something was definitely wrong.

"This is Detective Jones, Palm Beach Sheriff's Office Homicide Unit. I'm afraid I have some bad news about Miss Lewis and I'm having a hard time finding her next of kin. Can you come down to 12th Avenue South and "D" Street to meet with me, I need any information or help I can get with-"

"I don't think so..." said Lil E, hanging up on him, his eyes already tearing up as he immediately drove toward the Metro PCS store on the other side of Lake Worth to buy a new phone so he can call Grey Goose from a clean phone. He would have to toss the one he had, since police now had that number. He just couldn't believe someone had killed his beloved mother whom he had always adored.

He couldn't wrap his head around it. Who would want to kill his mother? and who in Palm Beach County even knew that she was back up here? he mused to himself. The same people who killed his father? he wondered. His head was all over the place at this time, but he would find out. That he *would* do.

Chapter Seventeen

Skyla

As soon as Skyla walked through her front door, she saw her daughter, Imani, sitting on the living room couch with her best friend Kesha. She closed the door and Imani jumped up and immediately came running to her. She naturally hugged her daughter tight, patting her softly and telling her that everything was going to be alright, trying to reassure her.

"Mommy! Where were you?" cried Imani, hugging her mother back in relief.

"It's okay, baby. Everything will be okay now, sweetheart," said Skyla, trying to reassure Imani so that she knows she doesn't have to worry about it or anything else for that matter.

"Are you okay?" asked Kesha. "I'm gonna go now. I'll see you at school, okay?"

"Okay, Kesh. Thank you for being here for Imani, you're a good friend," said Skyla as Kesha slipped toward the front door and silently left. "It's going to be alright, Imani. Shhhh..."

"Where were you, mommy? We've been worried sick about you. Kian got shot again, two nights ago. He's-" started Imani before Skyla interrupted her.

"Wait, what!" cried Skyla. "Why didn't anyone tell me about this? Is he okay?"

"Yea, he's fine, mommy. We *did* try to call you, but you left your phone here on the charger. He's over there at JFK and Jay and Isabella are there with Quan. They made me come home to wait on you-mommy where you been? We've been so worried! We thought-"

"You thought that I relapsed?" Skyla asked, cutting her off, heartbroken about her past, about what her kids must have been thinking.

"Yea, I'm sorry, mommy. But you just disappeared..." said Imani. "Oh, and somebody said they saw you with Nita by the corner store...I guess we just assumed. I'm sorry, mommy."

"Nah, baby. There's nothing for you to apologize for. But look, this is important, okay? Who saw me down there with Nita?" asked Skyla seriously.

"Mommy, you're scaring me! Why do you want to know so bad?"

"It's just very important, baby. You can't let anyone know I was gone, okay?" said Skyla.

"Well, I won't say nothing, but-oh yea, there was this cop that came by. I think I remember him from when daddy got killed...I didn't say anything to him besides that you weren't here, but he left his card," said Imani, picking the detective's card up from the coffee table and handing it to Skyla, who immediately furrowed her brow looking at it.

"Sweetheart, are you sure you didn't say anything to him? Nobody can know that I was gone-it's very important, Imani-" started Skyla.

"Mommy, I know better than to talk to police! I *have* watched Revolt's Black News show. I know they ain't there to help us, even if he was black..." said Imani with confidence.

"Okay, baby. I'm not even gon' ask you where you learned all of that from, but okay..." said Skyla, tucking the detective's card in her pocket with the intention of calling him later, but for now, she has to firmly establish her alibi before letting him corner her. "C'mon, let's get back to the hospital and check on your brother, okay? And if it ever comes up, that's where I was: at JFK medical center with your brother, but you are right about not ever talking to the police."

Skyla made her way out to her Toyota and they headed over to the hospital to check on Kian and pray with him to get better.

§§§§

As they walked into Kian's hospital room, all eyes turned their way. Most faces had a shocked look on them, but not Jermaine, her baby boy. He looked relieved as he ran to her, wrapping his arms around her almost in tears. He is the glue in her family, she thought to herself, a smile forming at her lips.

"Where were you?" Jermaine asked worriedly, yet obviously relieved to see her back, safe and with them.

Skyla only shook her head, No, before saying, "All that matters is that I'm here now and that everything is going to be alright."

"Ah, baby?" asked Isabella, looking at Kian. "I'ma go and see if I can find you some food to eat. Imani? Why don't you come with me so your mother can talk to Kian?"

Skyla nodded her head at Isabella gratefully, proud that she is so smart and perceptive. Once they turned and left, Skyla looked to Quan, Jay, and Kian. She didn't think twice about talking in front of Quan, because after she and Kian had made up and squashed their differences and Kian had told her everything that had taken place at Grove Custom Auto, the mechanic shop in Delray Beach, he had admitted to torturing and killing Sin. That was how Skyla had even known about her friend Nikki, and how she had set the whole thing up. But he also mentioned to her how Quan had saved his life when he had shot and killed the Y-Lo that had shot Kilo, and for that and some other more private issues, she trusted Quan with their lives.

"I need y'all to say I was here with Kian since he was shot two days ago and I need y'all to forget that I've went missing, no questions asked," said Skyla.

"Just like that?" asked Kian, obviously pissed off. "Where have you-"

"I said 'no questions' Kian, I'm serious! I need y'all to be my alibi and I've gotta call this Detective Jones since Imani say he already be done went by the house..." said Skyla, trailing off.

"Why is you finna call him for, moms?" asked Jermaine. "We don't talk to police-"

"Boy-bye with all of that mess! I'm too connected to the victim. I'm just going to innocently call so he just assumes that I know nothing. I'm going to act like I'm trying to call about your father's murder, then I'll act like I'm surprised when he bring up-"

"So who is this about, moms? We got ya back, but I need to know what's goin' on and why the fuck you would ever think talking to the cops is a good idea?" Kian finally asked point blank.

"Look, you just let me worry about this cop. I've dealt with him three times already and I know how he thinks and how to play him. I've dealt with him," said Skyla, with a confidence that she didn't necessarily feel, yet knew she had to reassure her kids and how to make this work.

"Okay, I get that much, moms. By the way why the fuck is homicide tryna talk to you? Who the hell is all this about? Be real, moms. This ain't like you..." said Kian, showing signs of worry on his face.

Skyla froze up. She knew that her son was in the game and knew he had been hunting his father's murderer for many years now. Oh sure, she knew he had killed Sin. But she also knew that Sin had only been the trigger to the gun. Nikki was always the finger pulling the trigger and the brains behind the plot. She had set the whole thing up. Skyla had started smoking crack, and during one of her enlightened moments, her deductive skills put two and two together and she had pretty much guessed why Nikki had turned on her. She wasn't even mad at Maniac. She knew he was known to drink too much sometimes. But Nikki had planned and carried out that plan. She had to die for killing Maniac. "I know, I know...Okay, fine. Listen, they looking for me because... because I killed the real one behind your dad's murder."

Chapter Eighteen

PBSO Detective Jones

After canvassing the area, including speaking to some of the drug addicts that frequently hung out around the dumpsters in the back alleyway behind the store. He had done his due diligence and come up with the big goose egg. Not only did he not even learn anything, but these were veteran street urchins, they refused to even speak to him. He was seen as the enemy. Always has been. He didn't understand it. Didn't they know he was there trying to help them? It was crazy, he thought to himself. He hated that the pop culture had made him the enemy.

People always complained to him about his solve rate in the hood as compared to the other side of Federal Highway in Lake Worth. The rich side. But when they, the black community, refused to talk with him, how was he supposed to solve these Black on Black crimes? Even when he *did* solve them, it was either the suspect told on themselves when he got them into the interrogation room, their baby's mama or wives told on them because of their cheating, or he busted someone on something completely separate and they agreed to cooperate to get off on their own charges. For just once, he wished someone would do the right thing. Just once he would love it if-

BRIIIING! BRIIIING!

His thoughts are interrupted by a call on his work phone. Checking his display, he doesn't recognize the number, but he had given out several of his business cards, most of which he later found crumpled on the ground, but all he needed was the right person to have kept it, all to call him once they were away from their friends. That was a break he really needed.

"Homicide. Jones," he answered curtly.

"Hello? Is this...I'm sorry, this is Marcus Hayworth's wife? Skyla Hayworth?"

"Ahhh, yes. Mrs. Hayworth, I do remember you. I actually just stopped by your house not too long ago and you weren't home, I-" started Jones.

"Yes, my daughter gave me your card. We were all still up at the hospital, so I only just now got your card. Worried sick, I left my phone at the house when I rushed on over to JFK yesterday...or was it the day before? It's been rough. But I had to return your call as quickly as possible, I definitely had my hopes up that you had some developments for me?" asked Skyla, a hopeful tone to her voice.

"I'm sorry, Mrs. Hayworth. You lost me, developments?" asked Jones, completely thrown for a loop, and not knowing how to respond.

"Yes, developments...News?" prompted Skyla, trying to steer their conversation away from the true purpose of his visit. Jones was at a loss for words and didn't know what to say, he felt kind of like he had lost all tact.

"You know? About my husband's murder?" she prompted him softly, clarifying it for him like a five year old.

"Oh, shit! I'm so sorry," he said, appalled and embarrassed that he could be so obtuse. "I really messed up. I am so sorry, but I don't-I'm sorry Mrs. Hayworth, I've been very insensitive. I wasn't clear about why I needed to talk to you and of course, you just assumed- I'm very sorry, but there's been no...there's been no new developments in your late husband's case. I wasn't clear, and that's my bad...Did you say you were at the hospital?"

"You-you mean there's nothing new? Then why...?" Skyla asked, trailing off and sounding quite hurt by his response.

"No. I'm sorry, Ma'am. Nothing new. Look, is it possible that I could meet up with you?"

"Well, I mean, I'm still here at JFK Hospital. But if it isn't about my husband, and now I know it's not about my son, so then...?" said Skyla, again trailing off and sounding cautious and confused, making Jones feel even worse for bothering her, intruding on her life again and bringing back bad memories and emotions. He obviously had not thought out his actions and what the implications to those actions might be, concerning this poor woman, who had already been through too much in her still-young life. He decided to kill two birds with one stone by driving over to JFK, verifying her alibi as well as apologizing for his misleading visit as he really hadn't foreseen this misinterpretation that was only natural.

First he was astonished when he first took in Skyla Hayworth and her new appearance. She was absolutely beautiful. Gorgeous even. It was in stark contrast with his memory of the last time he had seen her. Back when she had been a victim, hit in the arm by stray bullet that came from a drive-by shooting. She was an obvious drug abuser at that time, he remembered. Second thing he took notice of was the fact that she was now obviously clean, and doing well for herself by the look of things. Well, not entirely, he conceded. Her son was shot three times and laying in a hospital bed after surgery, so she was surely showing signs of stress and strain, but other than that, she looked amazing.

"So, you look a lot different from the last time we spoke," he said as they walked together to the cafeteria to get some coffee so he could properly apologize to her for getting her hopes up.

"I...well, I've been clean for over two years now. I guess I should be grateful for that bullet that hit me. It forced me to see the world I was living in. Then, once I saw it and I finally accepted it, I knew I had to change it. And then I just *did*..." said Skyla, becoming confident again.

"I respect that, Mrs. Hayworth-"

"Call me 'Sky'. That's what all my friends call me," she said, interrupting him.

"Okay then, Sky. I really do respect how you've turned your life around. I don't imagine it could've been easy. Color me impressed," he said with a chuckle to lighten the mood. "And look, I honestly didn't think first or I would've shown more tact when I contacted you. So, I do apologize for raising hopes, I didn't mean to hurt you..."

"Oh, it's alright. Shit, ever since his murder, I've been on a rollercoaster ride. That was my excuse to start using. Then everyday, being afraid to face reality is what would keep me using. But I'll tell you some real shit, after getting shot that day? I saw the fear in my kids' eyes, and it just hit me: If I gave up or died, it would be like serving my kids up on a platter to the same streets that took my husband...I wanna tell you something else, I might have gotten clean for selfish reasons, for me to be there with my kids, but I *stayed* clean for me to be there *for* them. Facts: They saved my life. Yet I've still let them down. Now, I've got a 17 year old son in there shot three times. No matter how hard I try, it's never enough. But I've got to still keep trying or I'll be letting them down all over again..."

"You're a really good mother, Sky. And I believe you're a really good woman as well. Don't blame yourself. Blame whoever it was that pulled that trigger. Of course it's not easy. This is Lake Worth so nothing is easy. But you are doing better than most-"

"How do you know?" she asked, sounding unsure of herself once again.

"Because I'm a detective, and I detect these kinds of things." He smiled.

Looking back into his deep brown eyes, she smiled back at him...

Chapter Nineteen

Jermaine

After his mother's big revelation, the hospital room had went completely silent. All three boys were stunned by Skyla's admission, unable to say anything. Then, as if on cue, they all had a million questions, each trying to imagine her being capable of taking a life. None of them could, but then after the Homicide cop came and listened to them all say how their mom had been there at the hospital for two days, they had left together. Jay had been scared for his mom, even though they had all played their parts perfectly to the Homicide cop.

When his mother established her alibi with Jones, he seemed to have dropped all concern about the Nicole Lewis murder investigation. He mentioned that she looked pretty stressed out and offered to buy her coffee downstairs in the cafeteria. Off they went after that, since it was obvious that Detective Jones was interested in her. As she was playing her role to distract him and minimize her involvement with Nikki, she had instantly agreed.

Jay had left after that. He had heard enough and had a lot to process. Plus, he had at least 20 missed calls and his girl, Jamie, had been waiting for him in the waiting room all day. He walked over to her and stepped into her waiting arms, hugging her so tight that he worried he might break her. He knew he couldn't though. She was stronger than anyone could imagine.

People always underestimated Jamie because she is so pretty with her blonde hair and blue eyes, and her skin complexion being very white. Jay laughed to himself over his brother's reaction to Jamie. He didn't even think Kian cared about her being too old for him. He suspected that it was because she was white. He knew it wasn't something as petty as jealousy, because although Jamie,

84

with her beautiful face, honey-blonde hair and slender, athletic body, lithe from running track, was plenty beautiful enough to be a swimsuit model, Isabella is nothing less than a goddess. But to Jay, in his heart, Jamie was *his* goddess. She is the *only* goddess to him.

"I'm sure he's going to be fine, baby. Don't worry..." said Jamie, as always, trying to make him feel better, even though he felt guilty for leaving her all alone in the waiting room all day.

"No, I know, baby. He's fine. He's just...well, my moms is back and-"

"I know! I saw her with some handsome, tie-wearing-" started Jamie.

"He's a cop, Jamie. Look, baby, let's just get outta here and get back to that money, okay?"

"Okay, I didn't wanna bring it up...ah, but everyone is blowing up my phone since you ain't been answering yours, and well, you missin' a lot of money right now. Everyone is tryna get right to go to Club Boca tonight, so...what do you want me to tell them?" Jamie asked nervously.

"Fuck it, bae. Let's go hit these missed calls and get to this bag," replied Jay.

"Okay, baby. Let's go..."

Jumping into Jamie's Jeep Grand Cherokee and hopping onto I-95, they were in Boca Raton in a matter of minutes. They first hit the dorms on FAU campus and got off on a lot of his already bagged-up product. It was easy. Once everybody knew that he and Jamie's faces had appeared back on campus, word spread and everyone lined up to get the best zaza in South Florida. This ended up causing a problem for both Jamie and Jay.

Seeing all the traffic, an RA (or Resident Advisor), who was a four-eyed, nerdy white boy, had threatened to call the campus police. When he, unknowing of Jermaine's skills with his hands, had attempted to place a hand on Jay's shoulder and physically move him, Jay had taken flight. It was as if he was beating up whoever had shot his brother and killed his father all in one. He two-pieced the RA, shattering his nerdy glasses and knocking him out. When he was trying to get up, Jay put him all the way out with a flying knee, expediting him right into dreamland.

Getting out of there as fast as they could, they ran out, leaving all of the FAU dorm students laughing at the hated RA who had gotten knocked out by a high school kid, something they were sure to roast him with for the remainder of the whole school year.

As Jamie was quietly driving, Jermaine was still amped up. He wanted to kill that fuck-boy. How dare that fool try to lay hands on Jay like that! Who they thought he was? he asked himself. Shit, I ain't no hoe-ass nigga! Mafuckas know that shit now.

He began to count his money in his pocket and saw that, along with what he had hidden in the kitchen overhead light at he and Jamie's apartment, he had Emelio's money plus a lot extra for himself. And he was yet to sell even half of his product. He hadn't told his plug, Lil E, but because of the potency and popularity of his product, he was going hard and charging more for his shit. It was still going fast. And he hadn't even started returning calls to his customers off campus.

As a policy he had made with himself, he always made it a point to call Lil E the moment that he had his re-up money in hand. It was good practice and he also was very grateful to Lil E for putting him on, giving him a chance, so he showed his appreciation by giving him the opportunity to come scoop his money even before Jay was done selling the product. So, he did so now, as per usual.

He hit Lil E's number on his contact list but was surprised to hear the generic Metro PCS typical "fuck you" sound off in his ear.

"MSL-zero-six, the number you have called has been changed or is disconnected. If you feel you've reached this message in error, please check the number and dial again," said the annoying computerized voice.

"What the fuck?" said Jermaine out loud as Jamie pulled into their apartment complex, The Vinnings, in Delray Beach, ready to pick up more work and then begin hitting their many missed calls off campus.

"What's up, bae?" asked Jamie, parking her truck.

"My partner...his phone sayin' disconnected. I don't-man what the fuck?" he said.

"Maybe it's a mistake," said Jamie.

He nodded, trying again. Same message. "No mistake," he said.

"Well, bae. We got enough for right now, don't we?"

"Yea, but-"

"Well, let's just get all these missed calls taken care of and do what we can do for tonight, and then we can do something about it tomorrow..." said Jamie.

"A'ight, bae. Let's go bag up and get movin'."

Chapter Twenty

Isabella

Isabella gets out of her beloved KIA Telluride, happy to finally see her dad's Prius on the driveway. She hasn't seen him for days. Since the day Kian got shot, as a matter of fact. The same day that she had been rushed to the emergency room and her dad had found out about her pregnancy. Of course she had been missing school, staying at Kian's bedside every minute of the day, leaving only to come home, shower and change. She didn't care about missing school since her grades were so high and her best friend Jenna, Quan's ex, was bringing her class work and homework every day when she came to check on Kian, so she could afford the absences.

Since all that had happened and how fast it had all happened, Isabella had yet to have a sit down with her dad about her pregnancy, which she found to be weird. Normally he would be the first to gently step to her, wanting to be there for her, showing her how much he adored her, no matter how much she had screwed up, or felt that she had let him down, he was always doting on her. But not this time. She felt so alone. She is scared.

Walking in the front door, she decided to confront *him* and then have their sit down, so she called out to him. "Daddy! It's me! I need to talk-" she started, but as she bent the corner and saw her father exiting from the kitchen, her words froze in her mouth.

She was appalled by his appearance and thought that he looked as if he had Coach luggage under his eyes, as if he hadn't slept in a week. He hadn't shaved, his hospital scrubs were full of wrinkles and his eyes were completely blood shot. He looked like a wreck.

"Sorry, Izzy. I can't talk. I've gotta work another double-" he started.

"Dad, you need to rest! Look at you, daddy!" said Isabella, interrupting him.

"Look, I know what you think. I'm not avoiding you, I just- look, I'm going to work, but we can talk later, okay?" he asks, trying to rush past her.

"No, daddy. That's not enough! I've been at the hospital- *at your work*- for three days now and haven't seen you one time. You haven't checked on Kian or me even once. Where have you been?" she demanded to know.

"I've been working doubles in intensive care, I have to make some extra money-"

"For what?" she asked. "You don't have to worry, daddy, you know Kian will take care of me and the baby, he is super-excited and-"

"Is he?"

Isabella froze up involuntarily. Her father noticed it too. He had struck a nerve. "Of course he is," she lied. "Why would you question that? You know he worships the ground that I walk on and treats me like his queen...Why would you doubt him?"

"Because I was a teenage boy once too and it's easy to get a teenage girl to fall in love with him, get her pregnant and then go on about his business. I've seen it many times before-" he started.

"Yes, I'm sure you have, daddy. But Kian isn't like other boys, he's mature, smart and dedicated while he also has a good head on his shoulders. He wants to be a writer. He is very artistic like me-"

"He's nothing like you, Izzy! He's a fucking drug dealer and nothing more! He will never be nothing more! You, sweetheart, have such a bright future ahead of you...as long as he isn't in it..." he said, trailing off as she began crying, pain ripping her heart apart knowing that the only other man she cared about in life doesn't approve of the man that she is in love with.

"Daddy! Don't say that! We love each other very much! He has my back and I have his. Don't ever say such hurtful things..." She continued to cry.

"Why, Izzy? Why him? Why can't you face the truth? He is no good for you. I've been there before. I know what you feel. The love. But the life he lives? The drugs? That will always be more important. When I was with your mother-" started her father again.

"He's nothing like Leticia! You chose a crackhead! Kian isn't anything like her! He's good! He would never leave me!" she shouted, cutting him off.

Her father shook his head sadly. What he knew, he could never put into words, but for his beloved daughter, he would try. "If he really loved you, he would leave you. Why do you think your mother did?" With that, he sadly walked out the front door, leaving Isabella in disbelief, tears pouring down her cheeks. Isabella had never thought about why her mother had left, but now, she had to look at it from another perspective, another reason. What if her mother had left *for* her instead of despite her?

She had a lot to think about now. This was something she had never even considered, but now she would. Why had everything just suddenly went to shit in her life? Weeks ago, she was happy and content, now things were coming at her from every angle.

Chapter Twenty - One

Kilo

After he had forced his girl to go home and get some rest, OG Dice, Glizzy, Quan and Haze had all come to check on their lil fooly. Everyone was pursuing every lead they could into Kilo's shooting, putting out the word throughout the whole ZMA organization and their combined networks of customers, plugs and workers. The word was out that the Big Homie Gunz had offered a $10,000 reward that led to whoever the shooter was or whoever had ordered it. He wanted him alive, although everyone knew, they wouldn't be remaining alive for very long afterwards.

Zoe Mafia Affiliates was definitely taking the incident seriously. Kilo was their golden jit and everyone knew and loved him. It had long ago stopped being about their respect for his father, Maniac, and become about their love and respect for Kilo the hustla. Whoever had made an unsanctioned move against Kilo, had in turn, made a move against the whole ZMA organization. This move would definitely not go unanswered. They had been going over it with Kilo for an hour now, and he was becoming exhausted.

"...just can't remember anything about it, y'all. I'm sorry," Kilo had been saying again, trying to deflect.

"What about the gun?" asked Quan. "Jermaine said he found both of the guns you hid and then maybe we can take-"

"We can what? Trace it?" snapped Kilo. "You really think a muthafucka who came to merk me-what? Like, used his own gun? Registered in his own name?"

"Okay, okay, bruh," said Quan, noticing Kian's recent aggression, even before being shot again and he didn't understand where it was coming from or why.

"Yea, lil bruh," said Glizzy. "Cool-out...Bruh just tryna think outside the box and find some possibilities. We gotta follow any lead we can, ya dig?"

"Look, Big Homie, I ain't wanna bring this up now," said Kilo, dying to change the subject. "But we got some bigger fish to fry right now..."

OG Dice looked at Kilo uncertainly. "What could be more important than finding the muthafucka who shot you and putting his ass in the dirt?" he asked.

"Okay, look OG," said Kilo. "Bottom line: Some shit happened and we might be getting some smoke from Calico-Zoe and dem niggas from Zoe Pound. I'm not 100% sure, but we need to stay on point with this shit... "

Glizzy spoke first. "You talkin' bout your Aunt Nikki, dem?"

Kilo only nodded, confirming Glizzy's educated guess.

"But we still ain't even found her yet, I've been asking around and--" Glizzy started.

"Apparently my ole girl found her, ya feel? How? I have no clue, but the overall point is that Nikki is a new resident of Hell and as a result, Calico-Zoe and Zoe Pound might be feelin' some type of way about it. We ain't got no way to know what they know-"

"That is...unless we *do*, ya feel me?" Haze interjected with a smile. "I mean, we still got my contact, Smooth, over there in Edison Projects. You know he dying to get down with us on our flaka connect. I can use that to get us in and maybe get some info about the situation- check da temperature, ya dig?"

"Yea, but that could also work against us too, ya feel me? Ain't he Zoe Pound too? Wouldn't he be obligated to let them know we barkin' up they tree? I mean, I know I would. So, what's to stop him? We don't wanna bring attention if they *don't* know. And shit, we can only hope she had other beefs..." said kilo, trailing off, starting to get a feeling of exhaustion coming over him.

OG Dice sensed this and decided they had imposed upon his protege enough already and stood up to leave. "A'ight y'all, we got enough problems to deal with, let's get going and put a plan into motion. Kilo, you get some rest. I'll be back by tomorrow when we know a lil bit more and got a plan ready. Tell your ole girl I said 'nice work'," he said, laughing as he lead the rest of the men out of the room to leave Kilo to his recovery.

Quan finally spoke after the others had gone. "You good, my nigga?" he asked cautiously, not knowing where his friend's head was at.

"Yea, bruh. My bad, bruh. I ain't mean to blow on ya. You my day-one, Quan. It's just a lot of shit goin' on, fooly. Shit. I'm worried about moms, bruh. We 'ont know what dey know and shit, I got a lot on my mind. It's all fucked up right now..." said Kilo.

"Yea, my nigga. I get that much. But don't take it out on ya fam, bruh. We just tryna get ya back and you snappin' an shit. I'll tell you something else too," said Quan.

"What's up, bruh?" asked Kilo, trying to let Quan get it off his chest.

"Bruh, I think you know who shot ya," said Quan, holding his hand up before Kilo could even start to deny it. "Hold on. I think ya know. But that don't even matter to me, I'll have ya back no matter what. Without questions. That's not the point though, my nigga. My point is that I think the Big Homie senses it too and that could be a prob-"

"Bruh, what is you even talkin' bout? Bruh, I just can't rememb-" started Kilo.

"Remember? Yea, I know. You've said that. But you almost showed your hand when you blew up about me wanting to find out the registered owner of the gun that-"

"Leave it be, Quan," said Kilo seriously, looking dead into Quan's eyes.

"I told ya, I'm always gonna get your back. I *will* leave it be. For you. But I am bringing it up cause OG Dice is not slow by a long shot. Point blank? He know you lyin' and I'm just tryna put ya ass on point. Da Big Homie knows something ain't right. Just be careful, okav, bruh? This shit is getting serious and I'm worried," said Quan, standing.

"I appreciate you, bruh. Don't even think I don't. You saved my life-" said Kilo.

"And you saved mines. You my day-one, my Z. I got you, bruh," said Quan, turning and walking out, leaving Kilo with his own tortuous thoughts to face, allowing him to make his next move his best move.

Chapter Twenty - Two

OG Haze, ZMA

OG Haze had just pulled off onto Congress Avenue, leaving JFK Hospital in his blacked out small body BMW X1 when his phone rang. What followed his leaving the hospital had been two of the most peculiar phone calls that he had participated in for a very long time. He had left his phone in his truck, already knowing the hospital's rules from back when he himself had been shot, but had seen that he had 12 missed calls from the short hour he had been inside the hospital visiting Kilo.

"Zagga-Zow!" he said, in his Ja-fakin' accent, seeing that it was his main man from Edison Projects calling and knowing he is half-Jamaican, giving him some shit about it as he always did when they spoke. "So crazy that you callin' me, Smooth! I was just finna call you, main man, I-"

Smooth quickly interrupted him in a very serious tone. "Did ya get that link I sent to you? I been tryna call you for damn-near an hour, bruh!" said Smooth, irritated.

"Nah, bruh. I been in the hospital, my lil bruh got shot up and shit, so I left my phone in my truck. What link you talkin' bout though, bruh?" asked Haze, wary, having never heard the nigga Smooth sounding so desperate before in all his time dealing with him.

"Fuck it, bruh. Look, I'm on the Tri-Rail right now passing the Lauderdale-nope, the Sunrise stop, so I'll be at the Lake Worth train station in like ten or twenty minutes, can you come scoop me?" asked Smooth.

"Say less, my nigga..." answered Haze, hanging up and heading that way.

Now, the other conversation he had to have was even more peculiar, and that was saying a lot. While on the first day he had been over at JFK Hospital to visit Kilo, he had inadvertently given Kilo's little brother, Jermaine, his number, in case there was any change in Kilo's condition or in case they needed anything or help for the fam. He had three missed calls from him. Yet he knew that Kilo's condition hadn't changed, since he just had left him there. He called the number back first, before even clocking the rest of his missed calls.

"What dey do, OG?" Jermaine's voice asked, sounding like the little kid that he was, although Haze had to remind himself that he was the same age as Kilo when they had put him on with Zoe Mafia Affiliates Family. He had forgotten that Kilo had started so damn young like that.

"What you tell 'em to, lil bruh! What's good?" said Haze.

"Ain't shit serious, I was just tryna see if I could bend ya ear on some real shit, and I know we ain't fo' these phones, OG. So, can I holla at ya on some real shit?" asked Jermaine.

"Ah...okay, check da play: I gotta meet someone at the Lake Worth Tri-Rail station and then I'm free, so you call the destination..." said Haze.

"I can come to you there if you want. I'm in Delray-so give me bout ten minutes, cool?"

"I got'cha. I should be done by then. If not, just wait, feel me?"

"A'ight, bet. See ya in a few," said Jermaine before hanging up.

Pulling into the Tri-Rail parking lot at Lake Worth High School, up underneath the Interstate I-95 bridge, Haze was bursting with curiosity. Jermaine, he figured, would want to get put on. He knew that had to be it. Maybe he would just front him an ounce and check his temperature from there. Little did Haze know, Jermaine's plan had nothing to do with credit, nor did it include anything as small as an ounce. He later found that Jermaine was going to pay-to-play. And he wanted to play with the big boys too, no desire to stay on a kiddie play-play level.

It was Smooth's call that was throwing him for a loop. What could be so damn important that he didn't even wait on him to answer the phone before jumping on the Tri- Rail and coming up to Palm Beach County? He decided to check for the link that Smooth had mentioned sending to him as he pulled up into a parking spot at the Tri-Rail and while he was waiting for Smooth and Jermaine. He was astounded after seeing it and reading the contents of the article.

The front cover of the Miami Herald had Calico-Zoe and quite a few other members of Zoe Pound all on a Federal Racketeering indictment. Plain as day- Future really had called it out when he put out "Feds Did A Sweep". The FEDs had apparently really done a sweep. The Federal Government was apparently asked to step in to fight the very violent street gang problem that had taken Miami by storm. All the gang members that the state couldn't deal with for lack of patience or resources had been passed on to the Federal Racketeering Division Task Force, the article said. Reading the rest of the article, he was astonished, but now he at least knew why Smooth was so desperate to meet up: If he could show up in Lil Haiti right now with weight on flaka, he would take complete control of the Edison Projects and the surrounding areas. Sorry to say, but the fact that Calico-Zoe and most of the Zoe Pound had been knocked, it meant that they had more pressing matters to deal with other than about his bitch's murder, plus opening up Edison PJs to Smooth, and in turn ZMA, was a win-win, sad as it was to see them go down.

His phone rang. After describing his X1 truck, he waited for Jermaine to come and jump in, since apparently he had beat Smooth here. "What's hoodie, lil bruh?" asked Haze, as Jermaine jumped in the shotgun seat.

"Man, just makin' it, Big Bruh. Man, sorry to bother ya, I-" started Jay.

"C'mon with all that shit, Jay. I used to be in the mud with ya ole boy, ain't no way I ain't gon' be there for his seeds now that he gone," interrupted Haze. "So, tell me, lil bruh. What's really hap'nin?" He looked into Jay's eyes to relay his support.

"Okay, OG. So, look, this is what it is. .." Jermaine said, spending a few minutes explaining his whole story and how he had his plug's re-up money put up, and he wanted to spend his own money separately to cop something exotic to sell at FAU until his plug came back online. Haze waited patiently, listening to every detail, all the while already having made his decision and knowing what Jermaine had planned. He was definitely impressed. Jermaine has a great business mind and is a hell of a hustla, he thought to himself. His daddy's son for sure, Haze noted.

"Lil bruh, don't stress shit, a'ight? Look, I'm finna handle my business with da homie comin' on Tri-Rail, then I'll get at ya. Look, save a bit of ya money. I got a QP of Grand Daddy Purp and an ounce of gas-ass moon rock for ya. Hit me back in bout an hour and head toward 57th out in Greenacres. I'll meet up with ya then, a'ight?" asked Haze.

"That's what's up, OG. I appreciate ya help, Big Homie..." said Jermaine, dapping up Haze, stepping out of his beautiful Beamer truck, leaving him to his meeting with Smooth.

Chapter Twenty - Three

Emelio

After a couple weeks had passed, today was the day that Emelio had been dreading. The day to lay his mother to rest and to say goodbye to her. He sat at her gravesite at the Opa Locka cemetery, while some Mexican men stood by waiting for him to give them the go-ahead to fill in the hole, burying his beloved mother forever.

Only Grey Goose had been invited to her funeral. Lil E didn't want anyone else there to secretly gloat, always having held animosity towards Nikki for being the Princess of Carol City's Haitian Cartel, so it was Grey Goose only, and even he was wise enough to keep his distance. Anyone else Lil E *would* have invited would've been close like family. But when the FEDs had landed their big indictment, almost all of the Zoe Pound, or those who hadn't already been arrested, had fled to Haiti to escape the FED's wrath. No, Lil E hadn't even heard about the FED's indictment until the last minute, but he still had already known that he was all alone in this. He had to find his mother's killer on his own, and he would.

Grey Goose walked up to him finally, after over an hour of him sitting at Nikki's grave and him worrying over his nephew's wellbeing. "You okay, nephew?" he asked.

"Yea, unk. Just peachy..." Lil E replied with some sarcasm laced in.

"Well, I know you ain't 'okay', nephew. I guess what I'm asking, is if you is ready to head back to Palm Beach County? Real Talk: Ain't much for us to do in Dade besides going to re-up. Edison's hot, Lil Haiti's hot, all of Miami's fucking hot. Let's get the fuck outta here," said his Uncle Grey.

As aggravated as he really wanted to be, Lil E knew Grey Goose was just being on point and trying to get back to the money. They both knew that it costs a lot of money to go to war. So, they needed to build their bank, arsenal, and their team's numbers up, because when Lil E finds out who killed his mother, he planned on killing their whole family, all the way down to their pitbulls.

"You right, unk. Let's go," said Lil E, kissing his Franco chain and Jesus piece, then dropping it into the hole and signaling the grave diggers to begin filling in the hole. As all the men were dropping shovels full of Earth onto Nicole Lewis' coffin, Lil E and Grey Goose turned and began walking back to Lil E's truck.

"Look, homie, we gon' find out who did this to sis and bag they ass, but for right now, we gotta stay on the job and we gotta get our bag up. Can you keep the streets fed for us? I guess what I'm askin', is if you got constant access to keep us relevant in the L-Dub? I got the clientele, but it's your job to keep me and our team fed, ya dig?" Grey Goose asked his nephew point blank while schooling him on the importance of it.

"Unk, the only way to get at dem niggas who smacked my moms is by stayin' in the streets and building up a bag. That's one thing you ain't gotta worry about."

"A'ight, and look, don't worry. I got everyone on our team out asking for info. Something will turn up and we'll find out eventually, lil neph. We'll find out eventually..." answered Grey Goose cryptically, sounding deadpan and serious.

Lil E got into his truck and turned on the Kodak Black and PNB Rock song that he'd had on repeat ever since he found out about his mother's murder. "*I done gave the jails too many years...years that I won't get back And I swear I done shed too many tears...some niggas that I won't get back Yea, I got niggas in the grave yard...Niggas in the state yard...I swear-not a day goes by...*

that I think the time- I wish that I could re-wind..." sang PB Rock on the song 'Too Many Years'.

§§§§

Later that night, Lil E had parked his truck at the old Lake Worth Flea Market and walked down 12th Avenue South until he came upon the alleyway behind the corner store and had been waiting ever since. He was ducked off behind the dumpsters closest to the back door of the store. It was because when he did his recon of the store, he found that everywhere out front was covered by cameras, but not out back. The problem was: That he had no idea when this back door would be opened, so he had to sit and wait.

For his mother though, he had amassed a great amount of patience, so here he sat, and would continue to sit, even if it took all month. The Arab would have to take out the garbage eventually, wouldn't he? So he continued to sit and wait. Lil E had fallen asleep, so he hadn't noticed that the store had closed, and now, at 5am, it was reopening. When he awoke to the back door being opened, an Arab man around 40 years old brought two bags of trash out back, one in each hand. Lil E quickly pulled his mask down over his face and cocked his 9mm Taurus PT111.

"Habib! Make one false move and I'ma put three in ya head like a bowling ball!" yelled Lil E after running up and pistol-whipping the Arab in the face with the pistol's front sight right across his brow, opening a large cut above his left eye, blinding him halfway, and fully scaring the shit out of him.

Lil E snatched him up roughly, half-dragging him back into the store.

"My friend! No money! No money! I just open right now!" cried the Arab, trying to plead to whatever God he knew, though it would surely be in vain.

"Shud'dup, Habib! I don't want your petty-ass money! Now, where the office at?" said Lil E, vengeance shining bright like LED lights in his eyes. The Arab relaxed just a little bit, mistakingly thinking that he wasn't being robbed or hurt, and motioned to a door next to the walk-in freezer. "Give me your surveillance from two weeks ago!" ordered Lil E.

"My friend! I already give to police! They have-" started the Arab, before he was painfully interrupted in the middle of the explanation.

BOC!

Lil E shot the offensive Arab in the knee cap and slapped him again, this time opening up a large laceration on his cheek bone. "I look like fucking police to you!" he shouted to make his point even more serious. "Open up the fucking Cloud, load the surveillance data onto this thumb drive! You think I came here not knowing that your backup is stored on the fucking Cloud? Do It! Now!" Lil E handed him the thumb drive then and waited as his shaking hands could barely take it.

The Arab finally got a hold of it, and struggled to plug it into the computer slot with all of the blood gushing from his face. That had been a bad move, but he couldn't cry over spilt blood. "Last 30 days instead, Habib," Lil E added calmly. Even struggling, the Arab finally managed to do it. He handed over the flash drive, almost dropping it twice.

"Please go now! You go-now, my friend!" begged the Arab, but upon seeing the look in Lil E's eyes, he grew more terrified. "No! No! Please, my-"

BOC!

Lil E interrupted his cries with a 9mm round centered in his forehead. Seeing no sprinklers in here, he ran into the store and grabbed a Bic lighter off the counter and a couple bottles of lighter fluid from the shelves in the back. He made quick work of it in the offices, concentrating most of the flammable liquid on the floor under the computer desk and the body. His purpose for this was two fold. One, to draw attention away from his motive: the computer. Two, to destroy the evidence in the computer and put all attention on the burning body.

He lit a paper on fire from the desk and threw it on the floor in between the body and desk to effectuate an even burn. He turned around and left before the desk even saw a lick of flame. Like a ghost, he was gone in an instant, leaving behind a fireball of Hell's doorway as a message to anyone who might have had anything to do with the murder of his beloved mother. They would never forget the name of Nicole Lewis.

Chapter Twenty - Four

Jermaine

Jermaine awoke and felt the euphoric feeling as she stroked him to his full length and took his dick into her mouth, her pretty pink lips wrapped around his 'Golden Rod', as Jamie called his dick. "If I wasn't already in love with you, that mouth of yours could definitely make a nigga fall, fo sho..." said Jermaine as she started humming, taking his balls into her mouth and stimulating them with the sensual, gentle vibrations.

"Ahhh, mmm-mmm," moaned Jamie, playing in her pussy with her fingers while still serving up Jay. Jermaine pulled Jamie up and onto him, so he could look into her bright blue eyes and pretty face. Genuinely in love with her, he preferred making love to her in the mornings. She smiled as she locked eyes with his honey-brown colored irises, her favorite feature on him.

"This is the view I love," said Jermaine, as Jamie lowered herself onto him, impaling herself with his girth and length, loving every second of his gentle roughness.

"And this is the dick that I love," said Jamie, moving up and down, riding Jermaine gently at first, but then quickly speeding up once her juices had fully coated him, and riding him like a mechanical bull at the El Toro Loco Club.

Her little tight pussy sheathed his dick in a perfect fit, gripping him tight with her pussy muscles, built by exercising with kegels on a regular basis. "Awww, baby, you feel so good inside of me, please don't stop," said Jamie.

Jermaine felt his toes curling as he watched Jamie's C-cup titties going up and down, bouncing with her movements as her pussy juice was dripping down his balls and onto the bedsheets, creating a puddle as she always does.

Jamie is a violent squirter when she climaxes and Jermaine loved every nasty drop of her. He was starting to go harder and faster, his balls starting to tighten up.

"Baby, I'm about to come!" screamed Jamie, also speeding up.

"Me, too!" said Jermaine.

He kept thrusting his hips and trying to go deeper as she rode him, his dick penetrating deeper inside of her, filling her up and stretching her walls. Putting his hands over her hips, lifting her up so he can control his thrusts even more, he pumped wildly in and out of her pussy, seeing her walls stretching, gripping his dick as it slid in and out, touching her bottom, deep within her.

Her body froze, her grip on him tightening, her tell tale indication that she is climaxing. "Oh Jay! I'm coming! Oh-shit! Oh-shit!" screams Jamie, barely able to breathe. Jermaine, hearing her cries of passion, lost control and let go, coming with her as they loved to always do. He busted his nut all inside of her as he saw her clear liquid come squirting, shooting out of her and down the length of his dick and his pelvis.

Jamie rested her exhausted body, allowing it to drop down on top of his and putting her head on his chest, listening to his heartbeat as she always loved to do.

"I love the way you wake me up," said Jermaine with a mischievous smirk on his face.

"And I love the way you put me to sleep every night," replied Jamie, her smile radiant and her face glowing with the after-sex joy.

They were very happy and why wouldn't they be? Jay smiled to himself. They were a power couple. Other students didn't have a bond as strong as they had together, most didn't even have a sex life as passionate and exciting as they did. And they had the exotic game on lock. Anyone knowing about or loving zaza knew to hit Jay's phone off top, because whatever strain he was currently carrying at the time, it would always be much better than what anyone else might have at that same time.

In the last couple weeks, Jermaine had continued to pump up with his many different selections of exotics that he was getting from his Big Homie, Haze. He couldn't lie, he missed dealing with Lil E, a homie his same age, who he also used to smoke and ride with, but ever since the day he has called and got the disconnected message, he never heard back from him.

Jermaine was still worried about his new friend. He hadn't been to school, hadn't been around the hood, nothing. His phone was still screaming disconnected. Jay didn't know his real name to look him up on Gun Club County Jail's booking records webpage or to even search the obituaries, which are two very real possibilities in the Lake Worth hard knock life reality.

Jay kissed Jamie on her pretty lips and reached for his phone. 18 missed calls already and he hadn't even started getting ready for school yet....

Chapter Twenty - Five

Detective Jones

Jones picked up the phone on the first ring, already in his car and coming back to Lake Worth from a home invasion-homicide scene in Greenacres, a town just West of Lake Worth. "Jones," he answered. He listened for almost a full minute before replying. "I'm on my way, I know exactly where you mean."

Detective Jones was now thrown for a loop. It had been a couple of weeks since the Lewis murder and now the owner of the store where she had been murdered had also been murdered and Rudolf Atkins, the Chief Arson Investigator had called him in to update him on these suspicious circumstances surrounding the fire that had been set there. Coincidence? he asked himself. Maybe. But there was a lot of coincidences that were surrounding all of these cases involving the people around his...what? he asked himself. Girlfriend? Friend with benefits? Future wife? He laughed at that one, but it was the irony in it.

He and Skyla hadn't put a label on their relationship but they were spending a hell of a lot of time together. It had only been about two weeks since the night at the hospital, but he knew it was something special that was developing between them. Shit, he actually *wanted* it to go far and be more. But he couldn't reconcile that simple fact that she might turn into a suspect at some point in the investigation, and today's call added another body to the growing death toll surrounding Skyla's associates.

As he pulled up to the corner store where Nicole Lewis had been killed, he could see no immediate fire damage, but could see all the water and soot running down the gutters of 12 Avenue South, tell-tale signs that Lake Worth Fire Department had indeed extinguished a serious fire inside.

"What do we got, Atkins?" he asked the Fire Department's Arson Investigator.

"Purposely set, they used an accelerant. Probably lighter fluid if the two empty bottles are any indication. There's a lot of damage, but do you want my real opinion?"

"I know you're Lake Worth Fire Department's best investigator and I trust your judgement, so yea, give it to me straight," replied Jones.

"The body was all staged to cover the theft of digital property in the form of information off of that computer- not the other way around, as they'd have us to believe..." concluded Chief Atkins.

"Makes perfect sense," said Jones. "If it was the killer from Nicole Lewis' case a few weeks ago, he would've done the deed right then, so we would've never had that surveillance footage to go on...how was this victim killed?"

"Well, the fire pretty much destroyed any evidence and hid any superficial wounds, but it couldn't hide the high caliber hole in his head," said Chief Atkins.

"So, a different methodology? Most likely a different killer as well..." Jones said, trailing off in thought.

"The computer and desk were burned more than the body though, hence my hypothesis," Chief Atkins reminded Jones.

"The killer didn't want us to know he messed with the computers. But because I've had that surveillance footage since the Lewis murder, he couldn't have thought that he was destroying evidence. No. This killer came to *retrieve* evidence..." said Jones, trailing off deep in his own thoughts and suspicions.

"For what though?" asked Chief Atkins.

"My guess? I think that they're doing an investigation of their own...and you know what? I don't think they like what they are finding out either."

"Who is, Jones?"

"Nicole Lewis' own people. I mean, who else had an interest?" Jones reasoned.

§§§§

Some couple of hours later, already late from picking up Skyla from her job at Humana's Health Building for their standing lunch date everyday, Jones' phone began to vibrate on his belt with an incoming call. "Shit," he said, as he was speeding along towards Skyla's job. "I hope it ain't no more bad news, got enough of that already..." He answered the call. "Jones," he said.

"Detective Jones? This is Brennan at Miami-Dade DEA office..." said the caller. "Ah, yea," said Jones, pulling over and grabbing his pocket notebook in case he needed to take notes or record any information on any of his cases. "Wha 'cha got?"

"Yea, ah...you got a BOLO out on a murder vic's vehicle? A dark colored Genesis GV70? An SUV?"

"I do- it's connected to a robbery-homicide up here in Lake Worth," replied Jones.

"Okay, we've got your vehicle down here at Golden Glades Tri-Rail station. Only reason we picked it up was because it was registered to a target in our RICO investigation into Zoe Pound, and Nicole Lewis is now your problem, so we will step aside now...Anyways, we *do* got your vehicle, but I'm sorry to say we already processed it and well, it was wiped completely clean- so you know. Just wanted to give you the courtesy of a heads-up," said the DEA agent.

"Yea, well I appreciate that. I'm not surprised. The killer stole the truck after the murder, so it only follows that he would make sure to wipe it good. But, let me ask you something out of my own curiosity- was the stereo system or rims taken from the car?"

"Nope. That is weird too. But nah, we have a fully loaded truck... I'll email you the details in our final report," said Brennan.

"Alright then- thanks, Brennan. We appreciate the heads-up..."

§§§§

Later on, while having lunch together, Skyla could see that something was on his mind, which was one of the reasons Jones was so into her. She was observant and in tune to his thoughts and emotions, and only after such a small period of time. A truly rare attribute in a beautiful woman in his experience.

"Tommy, what's bothering you? I can see you got something on ya mind...what's up?" she pressed.

"Aww, shit, Sky. I'm sorry, sweetheart, I'm not purposely neglecting you, it's just these cases are really bothering me. I know you ain't seen your friend, Nikki, in years, but I just found out that she was under investigation by the DEA and it's been bothering me that the pieces don't all fit together as they should, ya know?"

"Well, I'm sure you'll figure it out. Don't stress too much about it," said Skyla trying to reassure him.

"It's just weird. I have been dating you and feel..."

"What?"

"...feelings for you...and you were close to the vic. I don't know. It's just a whole lot. Then this Nita girl..." Jones trailed off.

Skyla stiffened. Then, realizing her mistake, she quickly relaxed and prayed Jones hadn't noticed. She took a sip of her water.

"Matter of fact, do you know a smoker named Nita?" asked Jones.

"Nita? I'm, um...I'm not sure. It sounds familiar, why do you ask?" Skyla asked, turning her answer into a question of her own and throwing him off balance.

"Aw, never mind, I'm just really thinking out loud. Sorry, how's your day been going, baby?"

Chapter Twenty - Six

Kilo

His day had finally come. He had just signed his discharge papers and Quan was waiting for the nurse to come back with a wheelchair, as per hospital policy that anyone signing out had to be carted out in a wheelchair like an invalid to avoid lawsuits. Kilo almost flinched when his assailant walked into his room wearing wrinkled blue scrubs and appearing as if he hadn't slept in three weeks since he had shot Kilo three times in the chest, almost killing him. He had never seen this man so unkempt. He was usually perfectly groomed and his scrubs carefully ironed and starched. It was an unsettling sight.

Kian scoffed at him without a sliver of fear in his heart. "Come to finish me off?" he asked, only halfway joking.

His assailant only dropped his eyes, saying nothing.

"Ain't it like against a doctor's code of ethics or some shit to purposely try to kill or hurt someone?" Kilo asked, pressing on.

"I...ah-I'm not a doctor...but you're right, I- ah...even as a nurse, I ah, violated my oath and my own code of ethics, yea. I, ah...I fucked up-"

"Fucked up, how?" interrupted Kilo, not giving him a break he didn't deserve.

"Excuse me?" asked the assailant, confusion evident in his brow.

"Fucked. Up. How?" he asked slowly, pronouncing each word separately. "Fucked up by shooting me-period? Or you fucked up by allowing me to live? Since I know that you know enough about the human body to know where to shoot someone to kill them...and you know where to shoot them to make it a serious warning."

Moments passed before he finally answered. "I'm not really sure, honestly," he said. "How about you, Kian? Why didn't you say anything?"

"I don't talk to police. Period. Point blank," Kian said, looking into those same familiar eyes. Always the eyes.

"You know what I mean. What about all of those gangstas that were in here on and off? You could've told them..."

"I could've..." agreed Kian, looking away and trailing off.

"But you didn't...Why?" asked the assailant again, as if desperate to know.

"I couldn't do that." He could give no more than that. It hurt him too much.

"Why?" the assailant continued to press him.

"I think you're pretty fucking smart. I'm sure you fuckin' know why, so why continue to fucking badger me about it? Why do you care? You obviously don't have respect for me as I do for you..."

"I want you to say it. Tell me why," pressed the assailant again.

Kilo sat motionless for a moment. He didn't see why he needed to say out loud what they both knew, but he decided to just oblige the assailant, hoping it would just move things along. Slowly he removed his hand from under the pillow where it had slipped after Kian had seen his assailant slide into the room. The assailant's watchful green-hazel eyes missed nothing. He didn't flinch.

As Kilo's hand was coming out from under the pillow, a gun was revealed in his hand. It was a smooth silver .380. A Taurus compact model. The assailant finally reacted, recognizing it immediately and completely surprised, thrown off his square.

"I wondered why it was taking the police so long to come and talk to me. Now I see," the assailant said.

"I couldn't allow that," answered Kilo. "I knew you would talk."

"So let me get this straight. From your point of view, I just tried to kill you. I saw the recognition in your eyes, so I know you knew it was me. But instead of talking to police, you hid my gun and covered up for me? You lied to gangstas so they wouldn't retaliate, and you kept my gun, why? I need to know why?" begged the assailant.

Kilo only extended his hand with the gun in it. He held it by the barrel, an offering. "Take it," he ordered. Serious.

"No."

"Take it, damn it!" demanded Kilo, beginning to get angry.

"You still haven't answered me."

"You know why," Kilo reminded him.

"Say it," demanded the assailant.

"Fuck! Because you are my unborn child's grandfather! Because you are my future wife's dad! Because no matter what you do, I would never hurt my family, and me doing anything in retaliation to you, would end up hurting them, and I would never put me or my shit before them. That's the whole fucking why of it! Are you satisfied, Nurse Perelli? Have I accommodated you enough? How bout you? Did *you* even think about what *you* did and how *that* would have hurt them?" Kilo demanded.

Isabella's dad could only offer a blank stare in answer.

"You didn't-did you? And you're 'sposed to be the adult here?" Kilo persisted.

"I-ah. I just...I was trying to protect-" he stumbled his words.

"And who will protect them from you?" asked Kilo before trying to hand him the gun again. "Here! Take this! If you ain't come to finish, get back home and be there for your daughter. She's had enough let-downs in her fucking life with her mother, she don't need to lose you too!"

Before Mr. Perelli could even react, Quan walked in, hand at his waist, resting on the butt of his gun yet seeming unsure, looking between Isabella's dad and Kilo. Kilo spoke up first. "Ah, hey bruh. Izzy's dad just came to check on-" started Kilo in earnest.

"I heard the whole convo, bruh," stated Quan, interrupting. "Give me that gun...I'll get rid of it for ya..."

Chapter Twenty - Seven

Isabella

"...ggrrr fuck! Man, you ain't gotta kill me... just take care of her and my child...don't shoot! Ahhh..."

"Baby! Baby!" said Isabella, shaking Kian and trying to wake him. "Baby, you're just having a bad dream! Wake up, bae..."

"Wha? Huh?" asked Kian groggily. "What happened, Izzy?"

"You were having a bad dream and talking in your sleep..."

"Oh, shit...what was I sayin'? I don't remember dreamin' shit..." said Kian, but still sleepy while trying to lie to her.

"You were sayin' sum shit about who shot you," said Isabella, a questioning look in her suspicious eyes. "Kian, I need you to tell me the truth..

"Yea, bae. I'm always honest with ya, I don't-"

"Who the fuck shot you?"

They had been holding eye contact until she asked this question and then he lowered his eyes in attempt to hide his guilty lie. He said nothing, unable to answer her.

"And you gave me shit about not telling you about the baby right away," said Isabella in anger. "Now who's keeping secrets? Huh?" She got up and out of Kian's bed.

"Always honest? Humph! Fuck you, 'Kilo'. We can't have a relationship built on lies..." and with that she was gone.

Kilo laughed ironically as he watched her go. "Never told on nobody in my fuckin' life, now I'm getting some shit for something I said in my fuckin' sleep...Ain't this bout a bitch.. ." said Kilo as he heard his front door slam shut in anger.

§§§§

Isabella hopped into her Telluride and bucked the speed limit to get to her dad's house in Lake Worth's Eastside. She kept replaying it in her head, over and over, until she was almost certain about her conclusion.

"...Ain't gotta kill me...take care of her and my child...don't shoot-" Kian had said in his sleep. It all made sense to her now. Kian's reaction to seeing her when he first woke up. Kian 'not remembering' who shot him; not letting ZMA retaliate on anyone; and just downplaying the whole issue to everyone. It all finally made sense to her now. How could he? How could he hurt her like this? she asked herself.

Pulling up to her dad's house, she noticed that his Prius was finally here in the driveway and that all the lights were off, save the porch light, which was always on at night. She was glad that he was asleep. Not only did she know he needed some much neglected sleep, but she also didn't want him seeing her being nosy in his home office.

Coming through the front door, not even dropping her Coach handbag, she bee-lined straight to her dad's home office. She suddenly hesitated. She was scared at what she might find. She had always had a distorted view of her mother, but her father had always resided firmly on a pedestal. This might definitely change her naive view of him that she'd always held. This could be the catalyst. Steeling herself, she forced herself forward and bent down to the bottom drawer of her father's desk, sliding it open. It revealed a Winchester pistol safe. She knew the code, her birthday, 0711. Her dad had even showed her how to shoot at Gator Guns in West Palm Beach and how to have respect for firearms. He had wanted her to be safe at all times, in case he wasn't home, knowing that Lake Worth City was getting worse.

Zero-Seven-Eleven.

The four distinct beeps could be heard as she entered her birthday into the digital pad while using her iPhone 15 screen light to see her way around.

CLICK!

The spring-operated door to the gun safe popped open. The office light came on, as if turned on by the opening door of the safe. Isabella was startled by the light, but straight mortified by the contents of the safe.

"Izzy? What the hell are you doing creeping around in the dark in-"

"You shot my boyfriend?"

"How do you-Look, Izzy, there are extenuating circumstances and I know you can't possibly understand it, but...Izzy? Are you...Are you okay? What's wrong?" asked her father, running over to her in a near-panic state.

Isabella was doubled over in pain, both hands covering her baby bump that wasn't even noticeable to the naked eye yet. She fell to one knee and held on, her dad running to hold her. "Daddy! It hurts! What's happening to me?" she asked, her face full of deep agony and confusion overtaking her.

"Hold on, baby!" he said, grabbing her iPhone and calling for an ambulance.

"Daddy," said Isabella, almost begging. "My baby...save my baby!"

As he gently lowered her body to the floor before she lost consciousness, she could see directly into the back of the pistol safe. It was empty. That was the last image she saw before fainting and being transported to the hospital, that was his answer to her question, and that's why the gun wasn't there.

Chapter Twenty – Eight

Quan

Quan pulled off from Skyla's house at just before 3 o'clock, trying not to be seen by Imani, Kilo and Jay's baby sister. Nobody knew or could find out about the special relationship that he has with Skyla, his day one homie's mother.

Quan's father was the head deacon at Grace Fellowship Church in Boynton Beach and also a sponsor to quite a few recovering addicts in the NA Program there. Skyla's kids all probably assumed that Skyla had just stopped smoking crack cold turkey two years ago after being shot. The truth was actually a bit more complicated than that. There was a whole story behind the whole ordeal.

After the drive-by that the Y-Los had attempted on Kilo had missed, Skyla had been hit in the upper arm by a bullet. Damaging her upper bicep muscle pretty seriously. When Kilo had dropped her off at home after she had been discharged from the hospital, Quan's dad had noticed and called Quan to go over there with him, as Quan's mother would definitely not approve of them associating with Skyla. One thing had led to another and Ouan had ended up becoming Skyla's unofficial fourth child and they had become close. Quan's dad might technically be her sponsor, but it was Quan that was her shoulder and biggest supporter.

So, when Skyla called Quan to come over, he came running. He never expected her to come to him with the dilemma like this, but she did. Quan had already disposed off the Genesis truck for Skyla. He dumped it right at the Golden Glades Tri-Rail station in Miami, but there was now another problem, and its name was Nita.

Having a relaxing lunch one day with her unofficial boyfriend, apparently Detective Jones had let it slip about looking for a possible witness to have some knowledge about Nikki's murder. He had asked in passing if Skyla had known a girl, a smoker named Nita.

It had been too close for comfort. Quan knew it was such a shame, especially after hearing the whole story from Skyla and knowing that she could've never pulled off that Nikki hit without Nita having her connection to Murdle. Nor could she even have found out how Nikki was back in town without hearing it through her relationship of her buying dope from Grey Goose. But it is a loose end, one that connected Skyla to the murder, so this loose end needed to be cut, and fast. No pun intended.

Cruising the Lake Worth streets in his rental Cadillac DTS, Quan recalled that Skyla had said that Nita had been hanging out lately on the Northside, over around 5th Avenue North and "K" Street. He knew she would frequently sell pussy on Dixie Highway or out of Sneakers Bar on 4th, so he confined his search between 2nd Avenue North to 7th; from "H" to "K" Streets.

At around 6pm, luckily Quan caught sight of an orange '73 Dunk dropping Nita off at the RaceTrac gas station on 5th and Dixie. She walked into the store as the Dunk pulled off, another satisfied customer apparently, as he saw the driver's mouth fulla golds grilling, satisfied and happy.

Earlier that day after seeing Pee-Wee from "The Raw", or what everyone called Riviera Beach, Quan had came up on some tins of some gun powder and figured that now was as good a time as any to try some off the wall shit, so he put his sinister plan in motion. He stopped by the Quick-Stop on 6th Avenue South after leaving Skyla's house and knowing what he had to do to Nita and mad about it too. Why hadn't this dumbass chickenhead just kept her mouth shut? he wondered to himself. She knew the danger of opening her mouth about life and death situations. She knew how rumors moved in the L-Dub. But no, she had to get high on the rock and run her mouth at how she had come up on a lick right after Nikki's murder. Now her fate was sealed. Right along with Nikki's.

At the Quick-Stop he had bought a rose stem, a glass cylinder, used as a crack pipe, and some Char-Boy which is used as a filter-type stopper in the crack pipe. He took the rose out, popped the end and pushed some tiny bits of Char-Boy in the stem. Then he dumped a lot of the gun powder in, following it up with a bit more Char-Boy to disguise and lock in place the gun powder. Knowing Nita's habit of slangin' pussy and smokin' hard, it had made the plan easy enough for Quan to develop and carry out.

He pulled his DTS up to the gas pump but didn't pump any. Once Nita came back outside, a Blue Bull malt liquor in her hand, Quan stopped her. "Hey auntie! You workin'?" he asked her with an inviting smile.

"Always, if it's fa you, suga," said Nita, smiling big and showing that her lifestyle had not yet taken effect, as her teeth were straight and her smile bright with Lauren London-like dimples in her pretty face.

"C'mon, I can't take you to my crib, but I know of a decent bando we can use right quick," said Quan, using his finesse and smiling back to set her at ease and play his trick-role to the fullest. As he drove to an abandoned house near 7th Avenue North, where he knew they wouldn't be seen or disturbed, he continued in his role. "So, how much, auntie?"

"Fo' you, suga? $100 for regular, and $200 for full treatment and you look like a 'full treatment' type a nigga to me! Whadayasay!?"

she said smiling, knowing she had a good lick with the way Quan dressed and carried himself.

"Fuck I look like getting half treatment?" Quan retorted, after pulling up to an isolated abandoned house on "G" Street past 7th by the railroad tracks and then peeling off two $100 bills and handing them to her.

Quan reached into the back seat and grabbed a folded furniture blanket and led the way into the bando unobserved. They went around the side and inside through the back door.

"Wow! Not bad! I never knew this place was a bando..." said Nita, already getting undressed and ready to perform.

"Yea, it's my friend's shit. Hold on- I need a quick hit before we gonna get to it," said Quan, pulling out his own handiwork, the pre-loaded glass stem. He then pulled out a sandwich bag full of about 40 or 50 rocks with his other hand, allowing Nita's thirsty eyes to get their fill of the day.

"Is-is...Is that some hard?" stuttered Nita, eyes almost bulging out of their sockets at the view of all of that dope he had. After seeing Ouan smile, she knew it was. "Can- may I have-" she started to ask him before he interrupted her, anticipating her question.

"Yea, baby!" said Quan, handing her the stem and the bag of dope, further lighting her greed and thirst ablaze. "We here to party, baby! Go 'head and hit that shit while I go over here and set up our lil' picnic blanket.

Quan quickly got away from the area, not knowing how big the blast might end up being when she finally hits it. Nita wanted a "blast" of hard, well she would surely be getting a blast off of this hard. Quan laughed quietly to himself at what was to come. He first heard the click-click of the lighter, then...

CLICK-CLICK-TTSSSS-BOOOM!

"AAHHRRRG!" screamed Nita, gurgling on her own blood as her whole jaw had been blown completely loose. It was hanging on by one side and completely detached on the other. Quan wasn't done, though. He walked over and squatted next to Nita's slowly dying body. Looking directly into her eyes, he watched her soul leaving her body. "That's right, Nita," he said as her eyes bugged on hearing him say her name like that. "Let go, Nita..."

She took a last look into his eyes, knowing. Then she silently took her last breath and faded into the abyss and her afterlife. After searching Nita to get his $200 and dope bag back, he found Detective Jones' card among her remains and left it in a very precarious position- an actual message for Jones to back the fuck off, thought Quan.

Chapter Twenty - Nine

Detective Jones

Things were getting crazy for Jones lately and a few weeks had passed by as he had been searching all over Southside Lake Worth for a possible witness named Nita. Jones was just pulling off from a pawn shop by 22nd Avenue South off of Dixie Highway after speaking with one of his informants, a local celebrity DJ, and coming up empty. Little did he know that more bad news was about to come and rain on his little parade of an investigation into the murders of Nicole Lewis and Abdul Abba at the 12th Avenue South corner store

BRIIIING! BRIIIING!

Jones picked up on the second ring of his phone, hoping it was one of his informants calling him with the whereabouts of his missing potential witness. He was correct on the latter and wrong on the former, much to his dismay. "Jones," he said, answering the call.

"Jones?" asked the caller, unsure. "Is this PBSO Detective Jones?"

"Yea, this is Jones here, who is this?" Jones retorted. Shit, you called me, he thought to himself.

"Okay, Jones, I don't think that we've had the pleasure of meeting, but I'm PBSO Detective Evans, I got something strange over here and think you need to come have a look..."

"Copy, Evans. What's your 10-20?" asked Jones, sliding easily into his cop lingo.

"I'm on "G" Street, about halfway through the block between 7th and 8th North-"

"Excuse me, did you say 'North'?" clarified Jones, since he normally only worked Southside Lake Worth homicides.

§§§§

Pulling up to a live crime scene, Jones put his name into the sign-in sheet that the Corporal had at the edge of the crime scene tape, and then he ducked under it, in search of Detective Evans, who was actually assigned to this case. Jones still didn't know why he had been called in on this one, but he was curious.

"Evans?" Jones asked the bald, well-built, brown-skinned detective in a suit.

"Jones, I presume?" asked Evans, shaking his hand.

"What we got?"

"Follow me- Oh yea, and Jones? Prepare yourself for this one, it's one of the worst homicides I've ever seen in my 20-plus year career..."

Jones followed him into the abandoned and dilapidated house and still had no idea why he had even been called in on this one, but he knew they wouldn't have called him in frivolously. As he followed Evans into the front door, his eyes attempted to adjust to the low light as his nose was overwhelmed by the death that had taken place here. It was a powerful and overtaking smell that completely caught him off guard. This body had been decomposing for a while apparently. Evans stopped by what looked like a heap of trash. It wasn't trash that he was seeing though. It was a small female homicide victim, and what unexplainable horrendous acts that this human being, this woman,

126

had been subjected to, Jones just couldn't imagine, couldn't begin to comprehend. It was simply gruesome.

"Take notice of the area where the mouth should be..." pointed out Evans.

Jones did just as Evans directed. He saw the eye sockets, where maggots were completely engulfed inside of the area where the eyeballs should be. He then lowered his gaze. The bottom half of the nose had been completely removed-or most likely blow away by some sort of incendiary device. The bottom half of the jaw was sideways and hanging barely by a muscle or a tendon. It was like nothing Jones had ever seen before.

Looking into the area where the mouth should be, there was a grotesque mess of macabre horror, Jones saw. He almost retched at the sight of it. It was unlike anything he had ever seen or heard of before. What in the fuck kind of sick and twisted mind could've even thought up some shit like this? he asked himself. He had another question though.

"Look, Evans, I admit...this is horrific and I've never-in all of my years... But look, why in the hell did you call me in on-" Jones stopped abruptly.

"This was found in that mess of...It was found where her mouth should be..." said Evans, holding up a clear plastic bag with red tape that said 'Evidence' on it, letting Jones take a long look at the contents of the evidence bag.

"Oh, shit..." said Jones, completely flabbergasted.

Inside the evidence bag, covered in dried and crusted blood, was Jones' official Palm Beach County Sheriff's Office business card and it was barely recognizable, yet they both knew that it was in fact his. So, Nita *had* known he was looking for her after all.

"Somebody's sending you a message, Jones," said Evans.

"So, if you can help me in finding out who that might be, I might be able to find my perp and get some justice for this poor lost soul right here who, God only knows, was put through this...Well, whatever this is..."

Chapter Thirty

Emelio

Lil E, Grey Goose, and the rest of their crew had been looking for Nita for over a week and had come up empty. Until tonight, that is. Tonight they had come across some most unexpected news. The first news that they had heard was when they had run down on Murdle and she had let them know that Nita was the only one who had asked to see their appointment book to "see if there was an available spot" that she could make it to.

Grey Goose had already knew who Nita was, so he had updated Lil E and they had all been on her trail ever since. The trail led to Lake Worth's Northside, a side that Grey Goose and his crew rarely ventured into with all the shit going on with ZMA and Haitian Sensations and now Zoe Pound. Everyone had been staying close to home.

The word was that Nita had been on or around 5th Avenue and "K" Street. Just before Grey Goose was going to update the crew and Lil E, he got the call from his sister's baby daddy's cousin, a dispatcher at PBSO he was fucking, who had also been trying to help them find this Nita. She said Nita's body had been identified as a murder vic off of "G" Street and that she had been dead for over a week.

"She got smacked?" asked Lil E, incredulous and pissed off at the same time.

"I ain't talkin' bout just murdered," said Jackie, the PBSO dispatcher that was helping Grey Goose with information for a little bit of a kickback. "They made her eat a grenade or some shit like that. I mean, I read that report in the database and I was almost sick to my stomach. Whoever did it though, they left another detective's card in her mouth that was blown off."

Lil E looked over at Grey Goose, determined.

"Who was the detect-" started Lil E, but Grey Goose tried to stop him.

"Lil Bruh, we can't fuck-" said Grey Goose before being cut off by Lil E.

"Don't tell me shit I can't do, nigga! This my OG we talkin' bout and I ain't goin' for this shit! I need *me-* for whoever smacked my moms!"

§§§§

The next night, after paying Jackie, and a few other deputy friends of hers, Lil E finally had a location on Detective Jones' girlfriend's house and was now cruising around the "C" Terrace block coming back around again in a circle, while trying to find an inconspicuous place to park and watch the house where he was sure Jones would show up to eventually.

Lil E had no real plan of action but he had two throwaway Glock 27s that were as dirty as the cop that had sold him the information about Jones. Cops have no morals or loyalties, thought Lil E to himself. For a little bit of chump change, there was nothing these pigs wouldn't do.

He sat there for a good hour and and a half before he saw something out of left field. Something so unexpected that he was frozen and unsure of himself. Lil E sat in his Ford and watched as a white Jeep Cherokee on rims with an FAU sticker on the back window passed him. The only reason it caught his attention was because it had looked exactly the same as the white Cherokee that Jay used to pull up in. With that same FAU sticker in that same spot as the Cherokee Jay was always in had. Fuck! thought Lil E. He's turning into the driveway of the same house that Lil E had been watching.

To be completely honest with himself, Lil E had forgotten all about Jermaine. He had forgotten about everything. School, football, his weed connection...everything. He hadn't even smoked in days. His mother's murderer was all that mattered to him.

Lil E was spending every waking moment and every dollar of his income from his dope- sold through Grey Goose-to find his mother's killer. Nothing else mattered to him at all. So, it was no surprise that he had forgotten to call Lil Jay with his new number and pick up his money so he can drop him off some more work. He most definitely planned on making that move now. And then finding what his connection to this Detective Jones was. Lil E was going fishing and he hoped to land the catch of his life.

Chapter Thirty - One

Isabella

When Isabella awoke that night, she was hooked to an IV and could hear the beep-beep from all of the hospital machines that modern technology had provided her. She was awakened by a dull but persistent pain that was in her stomach. She was confused momentarily before hearing their voices.

"...and she started digging in the backyard then burying the Oreo Cookies! She had seen it in a cartoon! She kept looking back there until I asked her about it and she said, "Daddy-I'm checking to see if my Oreo tree is growing yet! Ha!Ha!Ha!" said her dad, telling the most embarrassing story of Isabella's young life as he, and her best friend slash boyfriend both laughed at her expense.

She took a look at her man, his arm in a sling over his white and red Amiri outfit and Miami Heat snap back on his head. She sighed, then said, "It's nice to see you two finally getting along so well..."

They both rushed to her side. Her dad on her right, and Kian, holding her hand on her left. Both had bags under their eyes and worry evident on their faces.

"Sweetheart-" started her dad.

"Baby-" started Kian.

They all laughed a little bit at the awkwardness of how they were both trying to speak at the same time, both obviously being worried to death about her and her- "Oh my God! My baby! Is she...?" asked Isabella frantically, heart dropping and full of worry.

"Stop it. The baby is fine, there just- well, there's complications. Bottom line is: Sweetheart, you've got to start taking better care of yourself...you've got to take your prenatal pills...and we're going to start eating better-and we're going to *stop* smoking damn pot, young lady!" Her father turned to look into Kian's eyes then. "That means the *both* of you..." he added, holding eye contact with Kian.

"Yes, sir," said Kian respectfully. "I understand.

"You both are going to be parents now. I'm going to be here to help you, but you guys are both going to have to step up and make some sacrifices. The pot is one, another will be taking her to her appointments and being there to..."

Isabella listened to her beloved dad drone on, giving Kian a bunch of instructions on how to take care of her and what he needs to do to "step up" and how it's a lot of responsibility for them to have a baby so young. Her heart was swelling suddenly.

For Isabella, to have her father, the first man she ever loved and adored, to be here playing nice with her One True Soul Mate, her unborn child's father and future husband! It was like a sun shower on a sunny day. She couldn't be happier or ever ask for more. Yet she still had to say what was on her mind and what needed to be said, even if it could risk the serenity of this tender moment.

"Okay, you two. I appreciate that you are working together for the best interests of me and this baby...but we need to talk about what happened."

"It's okay, sweetheart," cut in her father. "You just really need to stay hydrated and pay attention to your appetite and-" started her dad, trying to side track her.

"Daddy!" said Isabella in exasperation. "You know what I'm talking about!"

"Sweetheart, I don't-" he started again before being interrupted again.

"Baby, what's this all about? What's bothering you? I'll do whatever..." Kian said, trailing off as he noticed her stubborn look.

"Okay, since neither one of you will speak on it, I'll bring it to the table. Then we will never again speak about it. What *you*..." said Isabella, looking at her dad before she said her next part, then looked over at Kian. "...did to *you*, will never happen again."

"Baby, look-" started Kian, trying to object before Isabella stopped him.

"Ugh-uh! Don't! I don't wanna hear it! I heard you talking in your sleep and- you know what? It doesn't matter. If either one of you want to be a part of *this* child's life, neither one of you will *ever* again try to kill the other one, okay? In fact, there will be *no* shooting at all from either one of you from now on, is that understood?"

"Yes, sweetheart," said her dad.

"Yes, baby. Of course," said Kian.

Chapter Thirty - Two

Jermaine

Jermaine had been burning up Boca Raton, and FAU in particular, with zaza and moon rocks and had really been doing well for himself. He decided to start studying, to take the GED test so that he could start taking classes at Palm Beach Community College before joining Jamie at FAU. He was really smart and his teachers agreed with his move to skip and go to community college being as though he was far more advanced than his contemporary students at John I. Leonard High School.

He put some "26 Forgiatos on the Jeep and bought a big Cuban link with a 7MA pendant encrusted with tenth carat diamonds. For Jamie, he had bought her a white gold Tiffany's necklace with his name on the tag. Jamie loved going surfing, so Jay had been secretly taking surfing lessons from Rusty, one of his zaza clients, in order to one day surprise Jamie with being capable of competing in a sport she loved.

Jay had been doing so well lately that he hadn't been thinking about Lil E's disappearance in a while now. Yet, it had always stayed in the back of his mind though. Lil E was the main reason Jay had got on, and he would never be able to forget his friend, even if only for that reason. Jay being the humble kid he is, he was grateful for Lil E's help, so that's one of the reasons that he was so excited about the phone call he received that Saturday night.

BZZZZ! BZZZZ! BZZZZ!

His phone vibrated in the cupholder of the Cherokee..

"Yeo?" Jay answered, cautious because he didn't recognize the 786 Miami area code.

"What's good, bruh? This Lil E.." said his missing fooly on the line.

"Damn, my nigga! Where the fuck you been at?" asked jay, sincerely happy to finally get back in contact with his friend again while his mind was soaring with hope for having his link back to better and more exclusive work.

"Yea, I had some family shit, so I had to be slide back to Lil Haiti for a while- lost my phone so I had to get a new one, then found it and got your number out of it, so I could get back up with you, just a lot of shit been going on, shit. So, what's been up wit you, bruh?" asked Lil. E.

"Fooly, I been pumpin' up cause of you, my nigga!" retorted jay, giving him props.

"Bruh, I knew you would Lil Fooly-"

"And don't even trip, I still got ya paper sittin' right here, no worries..."

"Bruh, I know. I trust ya...So, look, I need'a pull up on ya on some real shit an let ya know what da situation on da plantation is, ya dig?" said Lil E, dead serious.

"Okay, bruh, I'm in Boynton right now. Where you need me at, thug? I'm there..."

"Boynton?" asked Lil E, taking a moment to think. "Okay, meet me by the AM-PM store on Seacrest and I can get this shit off my chest."

"Give me 15 minutes, a'ight?"

"Bet. 15 minutes, bruh.."

§§§§

After saying goodbye to Jamie, telling her he would catch up with her later when he's done with Lil. E, Jermaine hopped in the waiting Ford Maverick and they pulled off, heading North on Seacrest toward Lantana. Lil E said nothing for a few minutes, trying to gather his thoughts while Burna Boy played on a low volume in the background. Jay caught 21 Savage rapping his verse on "Sittin' on Top of the World."

"Okay, my nigga," started Lil E. "I'm a keep it a stack wit'cha...I'm makin' moves beyond moon rocks and zaza. I'm doin' big thangs and you down wit me, so I'll let you in-"

"Hell yea, bruh! All you gotta do- pass me the rock and I'll bring us home..." said Jay, interrupting before Lil E could even get it all out.

"Okay, bruh. That's what I wanna hear, but you and I know that actions speak louder than words and I believe half'a what I see and none of what I hear, ya dig?" asked lil E.

"So, what you need from me? I mean, I'm ZMA first-" started Jay, showing his Cuban link and ZMA charm before continuing. "But I'm for you, my nigga, and I'm always tryna clock this bag off top."

Lil E gave Jay a strange look. "You ZMA? I ain't know that...I'm Zoe Pound," he said.

"Oh, yea?" asked Jay, holding out his hand for the Double Zees coalition hand shake.

"Yea, my Zee! I grew up in Edison Projects, so it was predestined I guess..." said Lil E.

"Okay, so obviously you got something on ya dome you need my help with, so...I'm listening."

"So, not going in too deep in my connections in the game, but I've heard that you got a connection or a way in with this detec...His name is Jones and I-" said Lil E before being interrupted by Jay.

"Bruh! Jones? How you...? Look, bruh, I ain't on no hot shit-" started Jay.

"Nah homie. Ain't nobody said you was hot. I ain't checkin' you, bruh. I legit need ya help with this nigga, he's got some information and I need to get at 'em," Lil E retorted back, reassuring Jay as to his intentions.

Jay was a little bit put off, as well as confused and shook. What could he say? He didn't like Jones. He was a damn police, not only that, he didn't like Jones coming around his moms and little sister either. But it was as if his mom was dating this fool, and Jay would most definitely never put his family in harms way when it came to his street life.

"Look, homie. I don't know how I could be of any help on this. The dude be comin' round my ole girl and sister. I've never spoken to dude and never planned on it. I'm really at a loss here too, cause I got no idea how you even found out about this. The dude don't come around me at all and even if he did, he a police, so I ain't tryna be friendly with him. .." said Jermaine in earnest, shrugging his shoulders.

Pulling over at Lantana public beach next to the Ritz-Carlton, Lil E pulled out a cherry blunt wrap and put some of Lil Baby's new strain of Wham in it, licking, sealing, and then sparking up the powerful blunt. He took a couple deep pulls on his Wham and then held it out to Jermaine. Taking a few pulls himself, Jay immediately felt the potent weed taking effect, calming and reassuring him.

They sat in silence, smoking. Lil E knew what had to be done, so he built up his confidence and just decided to ask Jay.

"I feel your position, bruh..." started Lil E. "But this situation I've got is very important to me, so I gotta ask ya...will you help me? I need for you to set him up for me and help me take care of his ass, ya dig?" He looked directly into Jermaine's eyes, trying to detect any signs of weakness, but found none.

"As long as we keep my ole girl and sister safe...A'ight, bruh. I got ya.. "

Chapter Thirty - Three

Quan

"So, did he say anything at all to you about it?" Quan asked her, already pretty much knowing the answer, yet not the details.

"I mean..." started Skyla. "He asked me if I knew her and all, but I didn't tell him anything. He knows about that period of my life- shit, he even seen me when I got shot that day, so he knows how I was into that life, he knows I could've known her but he didn't press me about it. It was more like he was asking mindlessly..."

"Well, ma, the nigga's a damn cop. I don't think he ever ask anything 'mindlessly', ya feel me?" said Quan sarcastically as he was known to do quite often.

"Boy-bye with all that shit, if he would've suspected anything, I would've known about it. He was just askin'. He didn't really think I knew her..." said Skyla, trailing off.

They had been at Sneaker's Bar in the corner booth discussing the situation and how Quan had found her somewhat 'boyfriend's' business card inside Nita's pocket right after he had watched her take her last breath. Skyla had originally just wanted Quan to talk to Nita, but after hearing the rumors of Nita hitting a lick in relation to Nikki's murder, Quan did what needed to be done with her.

They were now arguing about the disposition of Detective Jones and Quan was losing the argument as Skyla was appalled at the idea of anything happening to Jones.

"This isn't open for discussion," said Skyla with her best mom-like line, trying to end the debate about Jones' life. "I think-I think that

I love him, okay? I don't want anything to happen to him. Even if something has to happen to me."

"But Sky-" started Quan, intending to argue even further.

"Boy-bye, Quan! It's a dead issue, okay? I appreciate all you do for me, but I'm done talking about this shit. I don't want anything to happen to my man. It's a dead issue and stop worryin' about it, he ain't on nothin', okay?" demanded Skyla.

"Oh...kay. Fine. Whatever. As long as you're sure about it..."

Skyla's phone began to vibrate on the table. She looked into Quan's eyes before reaching for her phone. "I'm sure, Quan," she said, then answered her phone call. "Hey baby! Nah, I'm right downtown, but I can be there in a coupl'a minutes and I'll make us some lunch, is that-" She listened for a few seconds before continuing on. "Okay, I'll be right there...Love you too," she said, before hanging up.

"That was him?" Quan asked. She could only nod as she slid out of the booth and gathered together her bag and phone.

"'Love you too'?" he asked sarcastically.

"Yes, Quan," she said defiantly. "I love him, okay? Leave this shit alone."

With nothing more needing to be said, Quan sat there nursing his Rum and Coke, while feeling trapped in a maze. A maze of emotions, because while Skyla saw Quan as her forth child, Quan felt other-more contrary-feelings. He felt feelings that could never be reciprocated, but he could do nothing about that.

About the cop, though, there was definitely something he could do about that.

Chapter Thirty - Four

Kilo

A tear dropped slowly down Isabella's cheek as they were laying in the spoon position on the couch, while watching the end of the movie "Queen & Slim". A horrible ending as the incompetent Monroe County Sheriff's Deputies shot and killed both Queen and Slim.

"Fuckin' dirty-ass, puss-ass police! Damn!" said Kilo, starting to get up as the movie was now over. Noticing Isabella's tears, he stopped. "Bae? Are-are you crying?" he asked incredulously.

"Fuck you, babe!" she said, giggling. "It's a sad ending...I just can't believe that rat-ass nigga turned them in. It's just...Hey! I'm preggers anyways! I'm allowed to cry at weird shit!"

"Yea, I know bae, I'm just-" starting Kilo, before hearing his phone vibrate on the glass coffee table right in front of their L-shaped couch. "Shit, it's Quan, bae. I gotta take this..."

"Baby! You promised! No more leaving me!" said Isabella, pouting with her bottom lip out, looking as cute as could be and melting Kilo's heart. He kissed her bottom lip and answered.

"Yeo! What's hoodie, my nigga?" answered Kilo, walking toward the kitchen to get a drink.

"Coolin', bruh. Look, homie, I need'a holla at cha on some real shit. We might got a problem with this cop and shit...Well, look, I'm at Sneakers Bar, come pull up on me so I can lace you up."

15 minutes later, Kilo walked into Sneakers Bar with Meek Mill and Rick Ross playing out loud on the jukebox and the rectangular

centered bar only halfway packed. He looked around and caught sight of Quan in a booth and walked over to join him. Quan had a half-filled bottle of Captain Morgan on a table in an ice bucket. "Help ya'self..." said Quan, offering him one of the glasses on the table.

Kilo poured a healthy portion of the chilled amber liquid into his glass, then took a tentative sip. "I don't get how you drink this shit," Kilo commented, grimacing at the overpowering flavor. "So, what's the deal? You was talkin' bout Jones, right?"

"Yea, bruh. So look, long story short: He was searching high and low in Northside L- Dub for a bitch named Nita-" started Quan.

"My mom's friend?" asked Kilo, interrupting Quan before realization hit him. "But what does...oh, shit."

"Yea, exactly," said Quan in agreement. "So anyways, the bitch, Nita, was speakin' on some shit that got back to me, so I knew I had to deal with her before dem folks run down on her."

"What you heard, my Z?" asked Kilo, but already pretty much figuring what it was.

"Talkin' bout how she came up on a sweet lick at 12th Ave South store, et cetera. Basically, she brought heat down on herself and shit...So I body her and I found-"

"Wait-wait!" said Kilo, interrupting. "You smacked Nita? Why I'm just now hearing about this?"

"Bruh, you been having a lot going on with Izzy and the baby, being shot...So, I ain't want to bother you- I just handled it, okay? That's not the problem though. The problem was I found your mom's boyfriend's Sheriff card on Nita..." Quan trailed off, hesitating.

"Yea, and..." prompted Kilo, knowing there was more.

"Well, I left the card in her mouth-"

"What!"

"Yea," said Quan quickly. "Like as a warning, ya know? To back the fuck off and shit..."

"Man, why would you do some stupid shit like that?" demanded Kilo. "Are you *trying* to draw attention to ZMA? Why wouldn't you make it look like a robbery? Or a trick customer? Why make his attention even more onto the Aunt Nikki murder? What the fuck you got goin' on?"

"Man, a'ight...I know, okay?" said Quan apologetically. "I was trying to make it a threat to him- it backfired. Fine. My bad. On to the next. We gotta deal with him, bruh-"

"What?" said Kilo too loud, then lowered his voice when he noticed so many people looking their way. "Are you fucking smokin' on some flaka or sum shit? Bruh, we is *not* finna kill no fucking cop! Bruh, that shit would bring even more attention down on us."

Kilo took another big gulp of the foul rum and took a minute to think and figure things out. He had an idea. He didn't like it because it would involve the same woman he was trying to protect.

"Okay, look," started Kilo. "I'll holla at my ole girl and-"

"I already have," interrupted Quan. "She ain't havin' it, fooly."

"Okay, we finna go by there together and we will talk to her and come up with a plan."

Chapter Thirty - Five

Detective Jones

Detective Jones is sitting in his unmarked, parked on "C" Terrace in front of Skyla's house, the woman he intended to marry someday soon. He was not paying attention to his surroundings because all of his focus was on the ring that he was turning over and over in his hand. It was a rose gold band with a 1.5 carat princess cut diamond, surrounded by three-quarter carat baguettes to symbolize past, present and future. He was absorbed in the beauty of the ring he himself had designed and fabricated just for Skyla, the one he wanted to spend the rest of his life with.

Suddenly, someone was banging on his driver's side window. "Help!" a young black teen was begging. Jones dropped the ring to reach for the door handle and pulled. To his dismay and surprise, the door was forcefully snatched open and he immediately felt an unbearable pain in his neck, seizing his body, preventing him from trying to protect himself or getting away.

As Jones struggled to no avail, he was wondering who in the hell was dumb enough to try to rob a detective with his shield hanging from a chain around his neck. He then heard the passenger door open behind him. He couldn't turn to look though, as his body was rigid, frozen in place while the horrifying pain continued, but it wasn't for an extended amount of time.

SMACK!

Someone hit him really hard in the back of his head and put his lights out. Semi-conscious, Jones feels his handcuffs being taken from his belt and then fastened on his own wrists before he was carried a short distance until he was dumped on a ribbed plastic truck bed.

"Get him all the way in and close the tailgate and cap..." said one of his kidnappers, walking away. A door opened, then closed. Then Jones heard the tailgate close as his body was pushed in a bit roughly before the truck's bed cap was closed. Sealing him in. Sealing his fate.

§§§§

Splash!

Cough! Cough! Jones was suddenly awakened by a bucket of water being thrown in his face almost choking him on the water going down his wind pipe. "Arg! Wha-wha-are you fucking crazy?! I'm a fucking cop, asshole! You kidnapped a fucking-"

SMACK!

The same teen boy who had knocked on his window was standing in front of him with a huge gun in his hand. It looked like a Desert Eagle. He had a smirk on his face. He had- did this little mother fucker just pistol whip him? he asked himself. Yes! was the resounding answer, bringing his reality down to him. His badge was still hanging from his neck. This was incredibly bad news. Worse news was that he noticed how he was duct-taped down securely to a metal folding chair that he was sitting in. Bad news all around.

For one, this was no random robbery. He had been taken. Second of all, his badge hanging around his neck meant that this kid, whoever he was, *knew* who Jones was, knew he was a detective, yet still didn't blink an eye or think twice about kidnapping him and the fact that he was a cop wasn't even a threat in the least to this kid. That was enough information for Jones to put together half of a conclusion. He is a detective, so he was detecting. This kid, whoever the fuck he might be, is a dangerous motherfucker and shouldn't be taken lightly. Who in God's name *is* this kid? he asked himself. All he *did* know, was that he was in big trouble.

"I didn't go through all of this trouble getting you here to listen to your baseless threats. You only alive cause I need to know what you know," said the teen, still holding the menacing gun, his face expressionless. Stoic. Confident in his mercilessness.

The teen paused, yet Jones was smart enough to know that it wasn't his invitation to speak. Not yet. Jones knew the teen wanted some information that he possessed. He also could see into this kid's eyes, into his soul. He knew this kid wasn't faking. He saw a cold-blooded killer standing before him in the form of a school kid. Jones knew his threats were worthless. The idea of reasoning with him was equally pointless. Jones had to do what he had never done before in his life. He had to comply and pray for mercy.

"First of all," the teen started again. "Your card was found in her blown away mouth. A clear sign to me or anyone with a brain in da hood, that she was your informant and was killed for giving you information that you shouldn't have-"

"But-" Jones tried to tentatively interrupt, but was quickly shut up physically.

SMACK!

"Arggg!" screamed Jones after the heavy Desert Eagle was smacked across his eyebrow, splitting it and opening a faucet of blood running down into his eye and momentarily blinding him.

"I can see that you feel what you have to say is more important than what I have to say, so..."

SMACK!

"Do not underestimate me because of my age!" said the teen after hitting him again, this time in his cheek bone, which immediately began to swell up.

"Okay! Okay! Okay! Okay! OKay!" chanted Jones, placating his kidnapper.

"Fine then," continued the teen in a gentle voice, as if the whole outburst had never even happened. "What it comes down to is: I need to know what Nita told you. That's all. Period. You give me a lead on the one responsible for the Nicole Lewis murder and I'm gone. You'll never see or hear from me again and I'll leave your keys where you can get them cuffs off. Just give me that information I need and make it easy on the both of us...If not, I'll leave you to think long and hard about it."

Chapter Thirty - Six

Skyla

As she drove away from Sneakers Bar and headed back to her house on 12th Avenue South and "C" Terrace, she thought about how her admiration and appreciation towards Quan had sparked some kind of unhealthy fixation or infatuation he had started to develop toward her. She knew that it was wrong. But she had constantly tried to develop and promote boundaries with Quan, and he seemed to accept this, yet she still knew he had a little bit of a puppy-dog crush on her.

When she passed 6th Avenue South on Dixie Highway, her thoughts turned to her boyfriend. Yes, she thought to herself, I guess he *is* my boyfriend. She knew she was falling for him and she truly got the feeling that he felt the same way about her. He had dropped hints a few times about being ready for a committed relationship and wanting a family. She smiled to herself at that. It was exactly what she wanted. She was tired of being alone and fighting the world by herself.

She turned onto "C" Terrace and drove halfway down the block. She saw his car and his opened drivers door. She began to smile to herself. He was waiting for her. This was just his way of being considerate, parking behind her car so she wouldn't need to get up to move her car and let him out in the early morning hours that he was known to leave in.

Her smile faltered when she pulled up even with his car and found that it was empty. She was flabbergasted because it was uncommon for him to leave his unmarked unlocked with the Remington 870 and the law enforcement computer sitting right there in plain sight in the front seat. An uneasy feeling crept into her chest as her heart rate sped up, the worry starting to take over and her heart dropped out of her body. Something here is wrong, she thought as she parked in her driveway.

She immediately got out of her Toyota and ran to her front door, full of dread. She found the door locked, just as she had left it when she left that morning to drop Imani off at her friend, Kesha's house. No, this wasn't good at all.

Unlocking the door in desperation, she shouted out as she walked in the house. "Tommy! Tommy? Are you here, bae? Tommy?" She was running around the house, opening door after door, trying to find Detective Thomas Jones, yet knowing the effort was futile. He was gone. He had been taken. She could simply feel this inside her heart.

Skyla gave up in the house and ran back out to the car, praying, yet knowing he wasn't just in the car-ducked down-searching for his phone that he had just dropped. His phone! she screamed to herself still running back to his car parked out on the street. Reaching the car, she looked in and then poked her head in the back seat, yet finding the seat empty as she knew she would.

She ran back to her car and dug her Google Pixel phone out of her Coach bag. She hit the Send button once she had selected the last incoming call from "Bae". It started ringing, once, then twice and she heard the noise coming from his car. She ran over to his car in time to catch the last ring as his phone was vibrating on the street where it was lying by the front drivers side tire.

Her heart had dropped again. Something had definitely taken place here, but what? Now, that was the question she so desperately needed an answer to. An inner turmoil began to make its way into her consciousness and take over her entire being. Her fear for what might have happened to her boyfriend, versus her veteran streetwise gangsta-mentality about never calling the police. It was a deep inner struggle, but one side would have to win out.

The struggle ended fairly quickly, because as she looked at his car, a sparkle caught her eye, and right there on the floor board, was a ring shining back at her. She reached out and picked it up, immediately seeing it was an engagement ring, her heart jumped into her throat. It was a rose gold band. Rose gold was what Skyla had told Jones her favorite type of gold was when he had randomly asked her one day as they had been at Bryant Park spending time together. She smiled at the memory before the reality of what had happened snapped her back to the present.

It was then that she knew for sure...Jones had gotten that engagement ring for her and he had intended on asking her to marry him with it. She immediately cast aside her street training, her heart wrenching in pain, and she dialed 911.

§§§§

Some time later, she watched him as he approached. More arrogance and self-importance than the rest of the cops that had thus far been speaking to her. Some kind of superior officer, she assumed. His smirk said it all for Skyla. Another self-righteous prick, she could see.

"How ya doin'?" he asked without waiting for an answer. "I'm Captain Reider. I'm Jones'..Er, you're his...what? Girlfriend?"

Skyla only nodded, not having the heart to bring up the engagement ring. He continued right on, bulldozing his way through and crushing her heart. "Okay-here's how it goes-Missy. We're going to look at his phone records, his car GPS movements and his credit card activity-Hell, lady, we gonna look at everything but his bowel movements, and we will find who was behind this, and let me tell you, Missy: It won't be pretty at all for whoever's behind this. I'm just warning you-so-if there's anything you wanna tell me-an argument-a fight, he was cheating-anything at all, now would be the time-" the captain was saying.

She interrupted him there. "What the fuck are you...? Are you trying to imply that I'm some type of suspect or something?" she demanded, becoming very angry.

"From a law enforcement standpoint, we find that most domestic homicides, or 'disappearances'," he said as he stuck up his two fingers on each hand as air quotes for the word 'disappearances', as If it was a fake thing altogether. "...Are in fact committed by the spouse or paramour and even a family member sometimes-"

"I'm the one who called you fucking idiots to come over here," retorted Skyla, getting even more agitated than she already was.

"Now-now, I'm just asking. It's all a part of the process in our investigation and we are just doing our jobs, okay Skylar-" said the asshole captain, before she interrupted him.

"It's Skyla," she corrected, deadpan.

"I'm sorry Skyla...So, I just want you to come clean and maybe then-"

"Here comes my son. Look, you pompous ass, I'm done talking to you. Do your fucking job-and go find my fucking fiancé! Don't worry about me or mine. Just find Tommy..." and with all she had to say having been put out there, she turned on her heels, leaving the captain there staring gape-mouthed at her back having never experienced being addressed with such disrespect or condemnation as she proceeded over to a big, black GMC Yukon on big rims.

152

Chapter Thirty - Seven

Kilo

After the awkward talk that Kilo had just had with Quan, his day-one nigga, he drove them both over to his mother's house in his recently returned and fixed truck, leaving Quan's truck in Sneakers Bar parking lot. The drive across town to the Southside of L-Dub had been in silence, but upon arrival onto "C" Terrace, both of their thoughts were speaking volumes as they pulled up on an impossible scene.

"What the-" started Kilo in shock, before Quan interrupted him, pointing.

"Look, there goes ya ole girl," said Quan, relieved that all of the law enforcement activity wasn't because of anything bad having happened to her.

As soon as they had pulled onto their street, they couldn't even pass because of countless police cars and forensic vans being parked all throughout the whole street, looking like a street fair. Upon spotting Kilo's loud and unmistakable SUV on "28's, Skyla immediately turned away from the cop she had been talking to and began to make her way toward them. Since Kilo couldn't pass because the street was blocked, he put his truck in park and waited for Skyla to make her way over to them. When she finally got to the truck, she opened the back door and climbed in.

"Moms, what the fuck is-" started Kilo as he turned in his seat to look into her eyes.

"Kian-pull off-now!" she demanded, cutting him off looking overtly distraught. Kilo immediately did as instructed-no questions asked-because he had no desire to be near so many police anymore than the next man. He backed out onto 12th Ave South and drove West, toward Lake Osborne Drive to make a left toward Lantana, wanting to be as far from whatever scene was happening in their hood as he possibly could. At least until he could get some answers about what the fuck was going on over there.

"Quan!" yelled Skyla, punching Quan over the seat in the back of his head. "How could you?"

"What the-" started Quan, reacting to the assault on his noggin.

"Moms! What is you trippin' for?" demanded Kilo, pulling the truck over under the I-95 South overpass and turning around in his seat.

"You!" she screamed at him. "You two muthafuckas ain't gon' let shit be! Y'all can't just be happy that I'm happy! Y'all had to go and-"

"Moms," said Kilo, cutting off her tirade. "We ain't did shit! Just tell us what happened!"

Skyla sighed. Looking into his eyes, she knew that he was telling her the truth. She took a deep breath and began to relay to him what had taken place only an hour ago. "Tommy called me to come home-go 'head and pull off," she said. Kilo turned around and began to drive, allowing Skyla to continue. "So, he had been dropping hints about marriage and I believed he was just about to...No. He *was* going to ask me-and I have every intention of saying 'yes' and-" Quan interrupted.

"You can't be for real..." Quan blurted out. Kilo looked at him in frustration.

"Moms," said Kilo in a reasoning tone. "You can't marry some cop. This guy is the detective assigned to the murder victim that you-yourself killed."

"First off-he ain't just some cop. His name is Tommy. I'm in love with Tommy-the man, not the Detective Jones that you know...Secondly, he ain't never gonna find out bout Auntie Nikki cause there ain't nothing to find. I covered my tracks, right Quan?" Skyla said.

As Kilo continued to drive, he and Quan exchanged a curious glance, both of them at a loss of words, although for different reasons. Quan couldn't see why he could never be enough for Skyla, not even an option for her. Kilo was speechless because he couldn't understand how his mom could even talk to a cop, much less date one.

Nobody spoke for a few minutes, until Kilo pulled up to Rosalita's, an exclusive Mexican restaurant on Lantana and Congress Avenue. "I can't do this now," said Kilo. "C'mon, let's go get something to eat, and more importantly, some Margaritas to drink..."

Once they were seated, the waitress came right over, smiling especially hard at Quan. "Welcome to Rosalita's. My name is Angelica and I'll be your server today," she said, handing each of them a thick and handsomely bound menu. "Do you want to give me your drink orders now while you decide on your lunch?" she asked, as bubbly as possible.

"Just give us each, two Patron Margaritas at first, then bring us two more every 20 minutes after that, thanks," said Kilo, looking back to Skyla and nonchalantly dismissing the waitress.

"Ah, I'm sorry...I-ah, I have to see ID for the alcohol...um, sorry," she said, regretfully.

Without looking up at the pretty girl, Kilo brought out of pocket, a big fold of $100 bills and peeled off three bills, quickly handing them over to her.

"There's three IDs. Now bring our drinks..." he said, again dismissing the girl without even looking up.

"Ah, yes, sir. Right away," she said, walking away and pocketing the money.

"That was a bit much, wouldn't you say, Kian?" asked Skyla, as she was texting on her phone as fast as her little thumbs would go. "I just texted Imani and Jermaine not to go by over to the house, but we'll have to go scoop Imani from school soon-she gets out at three O'Clock."

"Okay then, we'll make this as fast as possible..." he trailed off as the waitress came back with their drinks and began setting them down on the table before grabbing her note pad and asking if they were ready to order.

"Just bring us that chicken fajitas platter..." said Kilo dismissively.

"Why you so rude?" asked Skyla.

"Listen, I need to holla at the homies about this... This is someone who followed him to your house and so I need to make sho' y'all safe and shit. What-" started Kilo.

"Kian," she said, interrupting. "He been staying with me there for-"

"Wait! What?" said Quan before feeling Kilo's look, and adding more. "I mean, well, I hadn't noticed that.."

"Anyways," she said, ignoring Quan's stuttering observation. "His car is always gone early in the morning, so Imani never noticed it, but he's been to dinner a lot too. Imani likes him too-"

"Imani's eleven! She loves everybody..." said Kilo, starting to call someone repeatedly on his iPhone and getting frustrated at it. He slammed his phone down on the table.

"What?" asked Quan.

"Jay keeps sending me to voicemail and it's really starting to piss me off. Look, we gon' have to continue this later, Jay been acting really weird lately and I need to find out why that is..." He threw a couple hundreds on the table and got up to leave, Skyla and Quan looking at each other in confusion as they followed him out, already knowing about his mood swings.

Chapter Thirty - Eight

Lil E

Lil E had left Detective Jones duct-taped to the chair for over a day and a half while his red nose pitbull, "Shine", had roamed all around the empty garage. All of his treatment toward Jones was a kind of psychological warfare, some shit he had learned from Haitian Sensations Lemonhead, who was incredibly smart. All he was doing was a tactic to get Jones to talk.

He knew Jones wouldn't take him seriously until he showed him how serious he was. So, after explaining to him what he wanted, he allowed Shine to roam free in the abandoned mechanic shop bay of the tow yard in Boynton Beach's industrial area, surrounded by other tow yards for impounded vehicles.

He was duct-taped from his arms and legs, all the way to his mouth so he couldn't scream for help. He had already pissed and shit on himself. Lil E could smell it. He was satisfied that he had got his point across and now had this Detective right where he wanted him. The Detective would have to take him seriously and would have no choice but to tell him what he needed to know.

Lil E had told nobody about kidnapping Detective Jones. Only his worker and new homie, Jay, had known about it and that was because Jay had showed enough loyalty and had the balls enough to help him pull it off. For that, he would always love and respect Jay. Very few would be willing to go all the way and actually participate in kidnapping a PBSO Detective just because Lil E had asked them to.

"'Mmm! Mmm!" moaned the Detective, trying to speak through the tape covering his mouth.

Lil E had tried to talk to this pig on the first day, right after he and Jay had got him set up in this garage and secured to the chair. He had refused to talk then, claiming he never even spoke to Nita. Lil E knew that was a lie because his business card was found in her mouth, branding her as his informant, and whoever killed her was covering their tracks from killing his mother.

Lil E waved his hand in front of his face as if fanning away the smell of feces and urine enveloping the beaten Detective. His eyebrow cut was infected and his left eye still swollen shut. "I see you've made yourself at home here. Just pissing and shitting all over yourself," said Lil E, laughing at Evans.

"Mmmmm! Mm! Mmm!"

"Yea-yea! I know, I know...you don't know nothing 'bout nothing-"

"Mm! Mmm! Mm!"

"Well, Detective Jones...we are sho' gon' find out what you know," said Lil E, unfolding some wires from around a yellow gun-shaped object. "This here enables me to put 50,000 volts of electricity through you...I bought it at the gun show at the fairgrounds..."

"Mmmm!"

"Yes, I'm sure you've used one of these on plenty unarmed black men. "

"Mmmm! Mmm!"

"Well," said Lil E, toying with Jones. "I don't agree with you there. I feel like once you put on that badge, you are a traitor to your race. You're no longer black, as far as I'm concerned. You're now one of them."

"Mmmm! Mmm! Mmmm!" Jones' eyes were bulging out at his inability to defend himself, but Lil E continued his monologue as if he actually could hear what Jones was trying to say.

"So, this is what's going to happen: I'm going to give you one last chance to tell me exactly what Nita told you and what you've done so far with that information-"

"Mmmm! Mmm-Mmm!" interrupted Jones again.

"Don't worry, I *will* give you a chance to speak-and I expect you to *speak* a lot!" said Lil E, as he unfolded the last of the taser wires, showing the needles at the end of the wires to Jones, allowing him to take a good look at them.

"So, if you *don't* tell me what I want to know, I'm inserting these taser needles into your jugular and running 50,000 volts though your neck. Then, if you still don't talk, I'm attaching them to your balls and well...you will know what happens then-"

"Mmm! Mmmmm!" moaned Jones, now shaking his head back and forth.

"Oh, if you *still* don't talk-you ask? Well, I've got something *really* special then." LIl E looked at his red nose pit, who was locked onto Jones' position, just waiting for the word to attack.

"See, without your balls-them being electrocuted off and all-you're just a bitch. And you see, Shine loves him some bitch-pussy! So, if you still don't talk-I'll pull down your pants and let Shine fuck you in your lil boy-pussy, ya feel me?"

"Mmm! Mmmmm! Mmmmm! Mmm!

"Yea, you right...cops are mostly faggots, so you'll probably like it too much. Nah, you know what I'll do? I'll order Shine to attack you and eat you one limb at a time, how's that sound? I ain't fed him in three days, so I know he hungry as fuck too! He's used to meat too. I never feed him no dry dog food either-he don't eat nothin' but steaks ...I'm sho' he'll make an exception for you though."

Chapter Thirty - Nine

Grey Goose

"Man, your fuckin' nephew is crazy! Do he really think he was finna get away with this shit? They already onto him! The only three cases Jones had most recently was the Danita Williams, Nicole Lewis and Abdul Abba and he already told Detective Evans and Captain Reider that they were all related somehow. So, just tell him to let Jones go! He trippin' fa' real!" explained Jackie, a PBSO dispatcher who had sold Jones' information to them.

"Why is you gettin' all excited about this shit anyways-" started Grey Goose, looking into her eyes while sitting at a hole-in-the-wall bar on Broadway in Downtown West Palm Beach.

"What the fuck you mean, nigga?" interrupted Jackie. "They been questioning me since he disappeared cause I was the one who looked up on the PBSO database about those cases and shit!"

"And what have you told them about us?" asked Grey Goose, a deadly serious look showing in his eyes. A suspicious look.

"Boy-bye! I ain't tell them shit! I said he called in to ask me about the tox reports and if the M.E. report had come back on Williams...Whether Reider bought it or not, I couldn't tell you-but they can't *prove* it's not true...Shit boy, what ch'all niggas done got me involved in man-shit! Y'all niggas had me thinkin' y'all just some dope boys getting some money and tryna go legit-but nawl! Y'all niggas kidnappin' cops and shit-" said Jackie before Grey Goose grabbed her by the arm and interrupted her.

"Girl-keep ya fucking voice down," he said between his teeth. "Just because you got some really fire ass head and good pussy-don't mean ya ass can't end up missing. Now, let me think..."

Grey Goose was really at a loss for words. He honestly hadn't thought that Lil E would go through with some wild ass cowboy shit like this. This shit is crazy, he thought to himself. Who da fuck kidnaps a fucking cop for no good reason? This lil nigga done lost his mind and went too far and I promised his mama I would look after him and get him on top of his game, but damn, this lil ass jit is more trouble than a lil bit.

Jackie headed off to use the bathroom after saying that she needed to freshen up. It gave Grey Goose some much needed time to formulate a plan. Looking around just to double check for any cameras, Grey was relieved. Seeing that Jackie had left her phone on the bar, he reached over and grabbed it. After removing her sim card and battery, he replaced the phone, hoping that he could distract her long enough to get her over to his house.

Jackie Bonafonte was a 25 year old beautiful Haitian girl. Her good hair, C-Cup breasts and perfectly round apple bottom ass were all natural with no surgical enhancements, so she had admirers within Palm Beach Sheriff's Office where she had worked as a dispatcher for the past four years. Jackie had never been interested in any of her co-workers though. Jackie was only attracted to thugs. One thug in particular too. Grey Goose was the only man that she had eyes for and his being 13 years her senior didn't bother her in the least.

Jackie had been in love with Grey Goose for years, and just being his jump off was okay for now, since Jackie had always known that he would fall for her eventually and they would be together someday. After meeting at Club Aftermath, they quickly got into a sexual relationship and had enjoyed the sex for the first couple years until Jackie's feelings began to surface, which had actually pushed Grey Goose away. Until recently.

Once Jackie got back, Grey Goose downed his cup of Patron, getting ready to leave. She sensed his frustration and moved close to kiss his lips. He allowed her to. "Look, I'm sorry, baby. Let's not argue, okay?" she asked him self-consciously.

"Alright, Jackie. Don't worry about it, I'll handle the kid, okay? Look, let's go spend some time together. Let's head back to my crib, okay?" he said in a reassuring tone.

"Sure, baby. Yea, I need some of that vitamin D you got anyways. It's been a long damn day..." said Jackie, now showing her beautiful smile.

As they walked outside and she moved toward her car, he smacked her ass playfully. "C'mon, bae. Ride with me. I'll bring ya back later, okay?" She only giggled in response, but walked with him to his rental. She never questioned him, nor did she check her phone.

Jackie was just happy to spend time with her man.

§§§§

Once Grey Goose pulled up to his house on Tropical Drive and 12th Avenue South that runs right along with the I-95 wall, where he had an escape tunnel dug under the 25 foot wall to limit highway noise, he led Jackie to the kitchen. They began to kiss and Jackie started fumbling with Grey Goose's A/X belt as she broke their kiss and backed into the kitchen chair at the table.

Sitting down facing him, she dropped his pants and boxers, taking him into her mouth. She began to slurp, and immediately bought him up to full attention. Knowing she had no gag reflex, she palmed his ass cheeks in both hands and rammed his full length into her throat, as she bent her head at an angle to easily take all of him while keeping heavy eye contact with him. Putting his hand on the back of her head, Grey Goose began matching her pace as she slurped all over his knob. She let go of one of his ass cheeks and cupped his balls, beginning to do her massage that would always bring his nut steaming down into her mouth. This time was no different. As he grunted, grinding harder into her full lips and warm mouth, he began to let go. His ass cheeks clenched as he sent a mouthful of hot nut down her throat.

"Ah-ah, shit..." he said as he climaxed. "Damn, baby, you do got that fire ass head. Now take off your shirt while I get some lotion to give *you* a massage you'll remember before we head to the bedroom and really get into it so I can make you do some screamin' for me..."

As he turned and went to the bathroom, she was her taking off her shirt and bra, her perfect C-Cups sitting high up on her chest as if proud. Such a damn shame, he thought to himself. She *did* have some fire head and some amazingly wet and gushy pussy. Shit, fuck it, he had no choice here.

Coming back into the room with her back to him. He placed the Palmers Cocoa Butter lotion on the table in front of her, and heard her moan her approval. He then took the Publix bag the lotion had been in and suddenly pulled it over her head forcefully and roughly. She immediately began to struggle, but his giant arms were too strong for her to stop him, she was scratching the fuck out of him, but he had a trick for that too. Finally, she suffocated to death and stopped struggling.

As an original KRAZE BARYE enforcer from Port Au Prince's Tabarre neighborhood, Grey Goose did what he was taught. Dragging her body to the backyard, he used his favorite machete to cut off her hands and head, his DNA being on both, and readied the body for later   disposal.

Chapter Forty

Jermaine

Jay had spent the last few days ducking and dodging Kian as well as his mother's calls until finally he had answered a call from a number he didn't recognize and got himself in a trap set by his intelligent and resourceful big brother.

"Yeo," Jay said, answering the call.

"Lil nigga-why the fuck yo ass ain't answerin' me and OG's phone calls?" Kilo asked.

"Oh, I-hey, Key. What's up with you, bruh? I-ah, bruh, my phone been trippin' lately and shit, bruh. My bad... I-ah, man-" stuttered Jay before Kilo interrupted him.

"Bruh, are you fuckin' serious right now? Why is you tryna duck me fo'?" Kilo asked, more to himself than to his brother.

"Bruh, I'm ain't duckin' you, I'm just-"

"Where you at, Jay?" Kilo asked seriously, leaving no room for Jay to wiggle out of.

"I'm at, well, I just had got out of school and-"

"*Where*!?" yelled Kilo, tired of Jay's antics.

"I'm at Jamie's spot, bruh... The Vinings on Linton, in Delray."

"In Del-fuck! Bruh, I'm on my way! Don't you fuckin' move," said Kilo before hanging up his new burner phone he just bought just so his brother would answer him.

§§§§

Once Kilo stepped inside of the apartment, Jay could see that he knew. Of course he would've noticed the rims on Jamie's truck in the parking lot, but that wasn't necessarily informative. But walking into the apartment and seeing all the Scarface memorabilia and expensive electronics, he knew. And Jay knew he knew. When he saw the ZMA diamond encrusted charm on Jay's Cuban link, it was all the proof that he needed.

"So, you sellin' dope now?" demanded Kilo. "You claimin' ZMA now? You wanna be in da streets now? Is that it? What the fuck, Jay? You got every opportunity to be a great football player and you throwin' ya life away like me?"

"Man, gone-on somewhea wit all that shit, man...I'm doin' me, bruh. I'm getting my GED and going to PBCC and then I'm going to FAU and-" started Quan, trying to explain.

"This all cause of that white girl, Jamie? This her work?"

"Man, this *my* work, bruh! I said I'm doin' me- so I'm doin' what I wanna do-just like you did! But, nah, bruh. I ain't giving up. I'm still gonna play- I'm just taking the fast track so I get where I'm tryna be at..."

Kilo stayed quiet for a moment, thinking. Jermaine took the initiative to try and go further in his explanations because he hadn't wanted his big brother, his role model, to find out like this since it wasn't a choice that he had made lightly.

"Listen, Key. I know how this looks, but I didn't just make this decision on a whim, I talked to my teachers and guidance counselor and most of them agreed that I'm advanced and can skip the last two years and go to Community college instead. I get one year in at PBCC, it will mean I'm three years ahead of those in my class when I'm at FAU playing football as a first string and the rest of my class are going in for try-outs...Can you see where I'm going?"

"Bruh, you got too much on you at such a young age...I guess that's my fault," said Kilo, shaking his head in disbelief, feeling the guilt hit him.

"Fooly, ain't none of this shit we been through-your fault...You ain't kill daddy. That's what all we been through stemmed from: The Y-Lo niggas that killed daddy, that's whose fault-"

"Jay-the Y-Los ain't behind killin' daddy...don't forget that Aunt Nikki was... " said Kilo oddly, bringing his mind back in focus onto why he was there.

"Yea, but I thought-" started Jay.

"Yea, nigga, Aunt Nikki had set the whole thing up, tryin' to take over daddy's territory, then she came up here with her son and-"

"Baby!" interrupted Jamie, walking into the room with a phone in her hand. "Oh, hey, Kian-Jay, you got Lil E on the phone for you..." She walked up, handing him the phone.

Kilo suddenly stiffened, finally realizing what had been going on all the while. As Jay took the phone, Kilo mouthed to him so the caller couldn't hear him, "find out where he at."

Jay looked at Kilo with a perplexed and curious facial expression, but nodded.

"Yeo, bruh. What's hoodie?" asked Jay, trying to act all nonchalant, but actually really shook on the inside because he had no idea what was transpiring here or how his brother even knew he was getting his dope from Lil E in the first place.

After listening for a bit, Jermaine spoke into the phone. "A'ight, bruh. I'ma be there in a lil bit man, just hold up till I get there, bruh. I got you!" said Jay, hanging up the phone and looking over towards Kian, a questioning look written all over his face since he had no idea what the hell was going on. "Bruh, what the fuck is that all about? How the fuck you know I was getting work from Lil E?"

"Listen up, Jay. Lil E was the name they gave to me in Lil Haiti for Aunt Nikki's son! This lil nigga been playin' you and I don't know why. I doubt that he knows our OG killed his, but he's definitely plotting something and-" Kilo started to explain before Jay interrupted.

"Wait, I know our moms killed Aunt Nikki...and Nikki got our ole boy killed, but why?" asked Jay, truly confused.

"Bruh, that's the part I don't get. But it makes perfect sense on why he might have went after Jones, because Jones was investigating moms for Aunt Nikki's murder-so we need to get at this Lil E nigga and see if he got Jones-cause our ole girl is going ballistic about this cop-nigga and I can't-"

"Bruh," Jay interrupted again, looking somewhat guilty and ashamed about what he had done. "I know where Jones is. Lil E there with him now, that's why he called-"

"So, where is-Wait! How the fuck you know about Jones and where he at? What the fuck you got goin', fooly?" asked Kilo, as the realization began to dawn on him. "Nah, bruh. Tell me you ain't got down with this lil nigga on a cop!"

"Sorry, bruh. I had to do it to keep Imani and the ole girl safe! At least, I was there with him to be sure. Look, bruh, he was finna do it either way. At least I was able to make sho ain't nobody on our side get hurt... "

Chapter Forty - One

OG Haze, ZMA

"Hit his ass again, Z!" Haze ordered Baby Boy, who was his newest member of ZMA and also possibly the most vicious with his hands and legs. Baby Boy, who was already out of breath-having been putting in work on Big Rico for almost an hour now, smiled at Rico, knowing what he was doing with his body blows. Baby Boy hit him with a four punch combination to his solar plexus, followed by two kicks to his ribs, which had been left open by his hands having been flex-tied to the water pipe above him in Baby Boy's garage on South "M" Street, where nobody would be able to hear the screams.

"Ahh-Fuck!" screamed the tough-ass Y-Lo hostage, knowing he was dead either way, so deciding to keep it gangsta and never fold on his fellow Y-Lo homies, who had noticeably thinned in numbers ever since the ZMA had crashed their party at Grove Custom Auto mechanic shop only two years ago. The majority who weren't killed in the onslaught went back to the Allapattah neighborhood they had originated from in Miami.

Really these past couple years had been kind of calm since the Y-Los really had no numbers anymore and had stopped all advances on ZMA territory and customers. ZMA had already been prospering and doing well, but ever since Smooth had become a major player in Edison Projects after the big hit the Zoe Pound had sustained, they were really soaring.

When the big Federal indictment had fell down on Zoe Pound, it had created a vacuum for a connect to supply the whole of Edison Projects, on all types of drugs, but the biggest lane they needed filled was for flaka. OG Guns had okayed the flaka being sold exclusively to Smooth, in order to keep Lil Haiti's Edison Projects fed. It was over a million dollar a month endeavor for the Big Homies, so of course they had all the lil niggas as security and making sure that the money machine kept flowing.

The new influx of money rejuvenated ZMA after the losses they had suffered while being at war with the Y-Los two years ago. It allowed them to not only expand their territory South into Lantana and Boynton Beach, but also gave them more resources to accept and feed hundreds of new recruits into their organization. New recruits such as Baby Boy, their hardest hitter.

All this new power and energy had also given them the ability to...from time to time...pick up stray Y-Lo members and question them about the shooting of the ZMA Golden Boy. Of course, they would also kill and dispose of these Y-Lo members after their interrogation as well, and that was well known by this particular Y-Lo staring back defiantly at them, refusing to answer any of their questions or even give his rank or set, as was common during these interrogations.

"So... you a lil tough-ass 'oye', huh? A real gangsta-ass paintcho..." said Haze, simply toying with his captive now, already correctly assuming that he would give up nothing. "All you gotta do is give me a name and the beating stops...don't even have to be your shot-caller, just give me your trigger-man and you got ten racks and your freedom, just-"

"Fuck you, puss-ass ITIANO!" he screamed and then spat at OG Haze, hitting his Giorgio Armani shirt with blood from his bleeding lips and missing front tooth, knocked out by Baby Boy.

"Baby Boy, what did you wanna be when you grew up?" asked Haze, ignoring the blood running down the now-ruined designer shirt as he calmly walked over to Baby Boy's tool chest and began rummaging around until he found what he was searching for.

"Me, Haze? I wanted to be a gynecologist. I always loved pussy," Baby Boy said, laughing as he caught his breath, not sure where the OG was going with this.

"Well, me, gentlemen?" said Haze, holding up the pliers in his hand menacingly. "I always wanted to be a fucking dentist-I always had a thing for the tooth fairy, so let's see how good I would be and bring her some teeth. Baby Boy, help him to 'open wide'."

Baby Boy grabbed the Y-Lo's jaw with one hand and put his thumb and index finger of his other over his nose, forcing his mouth open, as Haze gripped his left K-9 tooth and twisted and turned it amid the Y-Lo's screams of pain and agony.

"Ahh! Fuck! Arg! Ahhhh!"

Finally, the tooth came out, pulled all the way from the root, causing the Y-Lo's mouth to gush blood down his chin and onto his chest.

"I-swear-I-swear-I-swear-I-swear!" yelled the Y-Lo. "I-swear-to-God-I-don't-know!"

"Well, I'm not sure I really believe you...Baby Boy? Another?" said Haze, starting back towards his victim, still extremely pissed off about his favorite Armani shirt. His own phone began vibrating, halting him in his work. He took the latex gloves off his hands and reached to answer his phone.

Seeing it was Kilo, he quickly answered it. "Hey kid. I was just here talking about you. I'm with a friend at the dentist's office and-" started Haze before Kilo politely interrupted him with his urgent information.

"It's work call, Big Homie. Where's Dice? I can't get him on the line," said Kilo seriously.

"Wha-well, ya know Big Bruh still in Port Au Prince, dealing with that 400 Mawazo shit and won't be back till next week, but what's good? Lace my boots, nigga!" said Haze, walking off from Baby Boy and his Y-Lo captive.

"Yea, OG, this shit real and it involves a kidnapped cop-"

"A kidnapped cop? Nigga, what the fuck going on?" interrupted Haze.

"Remember that lil demonstration we all spoke about at JFK hospital?" asked Kilo, reminding him about it all.

"Yea, of course. I been on that shit since-shit, I'm on it now..."

"Well, I think the lil nigga who shot me, also kidnapped my ole girl's boyfriend...a cop," Kilo said, lying about who shot him.

"Oh, shit, Kilo," said Haze hesitantly. "Your ole girl fuckin' wit a cop?"

"Yea, my Z, but it's all good. I'll understand if the Z's can't help-"

"Can't help-nigga bite yo damn tongue! You ZMA lil homie, we always down to go to war for ya, it's just a lil weird, I mean...shit. What are we goin' to end up doin' with this cop? That's all I'm sayin'-shit. Never thought I'd be...well, shit, let's get it, lil homie, text me the addy! I'll call Glizzy-dem. Shit-Luna too, fuck it!"

"A'ight, Big Homie, see ya soon..." Kilo disconnected.

"What's up, Big Homie?" asked Baby Boy with a worried look.

Haze pulled out his throw-away revolver, walked up to the Y-Lo and said nothing before putting a bullet in his head. "Work call-nigga! Call all the homies...we gotta ride on da niggas who shot Kilo...

Chapter Forty - Two

Lil E

Lil E had only just started to beat on Jones and was already tired from the work he was putting in. He decided that he might get better results using electricity. So, he took the taser needles and stabbed both of them right into Jones' jugular vein, preparing to begin the electro-shock therapy that he knew would bring the results he was looking for.

Right before he began, he heard tires crunching on the gravel that made up the whole tow lot's ground. Lil E set down his taser as Jones moaned in pain and went into the front reception area of the long closed Atlantic Towing's office area and peeked out of the window. Must be Grey Goose, Lil E thought to himself, having been waiting for his Uncle Grey to get there after receiving a very cryptic call insinuating that Lil E had a problem in his operation.

Grey Goose and two other very serious looking men had gotten out of Grey's rental. Marquis and Buba. Infamous shooters from Haitian Sensations that were known to rock with Lil E's uncle. Nothing about them showing up with Grey Goose was out of the ordinary, but still, something was setting off Lil E's street senses. He felt something unsettling, but opened the door for them nonetheless. They all still technically worked for him. He was the S.O.S., or source of supply, as he had all the plugs for the dope at the absolute lowest possible prices. They needed him.

"What's hoodie, my Z?" asked Lil E, dapping them up as they came in.

"Zee's up, nephew. Just got us a lil problem concerning the cop..." said Grey Goose.

"Talk to me, Grey..."

"Well, my Z, it seems you fucked up with this cop-" started Grey Goose before being cut off by Marquis and Buba, both pulling out their fire on Lil E, pointing their guns at his head.

"Bruh, what the fuck y'all doin?! I'm muthafuckin' Zoe Pound gangsta! Y'all kill me, bruh y'all finna starve! Da plugs won't deal with nobody but me!" exclaimed Lil E.

"Yea, about that..." started Grey Goose, formulating his sad response. "Sorry Nephew. But we all way past that now, bruh. Apparently, PBSO already looking for ya. You be done fucked up somewhere along the line, Lil E, and you brought them peoples down on all of us. Haitian Sensations can't take the risk that you might not hold court in the streets. Haitian Sensations ain't takin' no shorts and no losses. I'm sorry, lil bruh, I really am. It's a fucked up situation, but-"

"You know Zoe Pound will avenge me! Y'all niggas dead men walkin'!" spat Lil E, trying to point out what was obvious to him, yet still accepting his death in the same breath and moment, while ready to join his mother and father in the afterlife.

"Yea, it ain't goin' nowhere...Calico-Zoe, all of Zoe Pound really, been in Federal custody under RICO indictment and Edison Projects are looking like a ghost town...Zoe Pound is finished and you were the last remaining link to a time long passed, " said Grey.

"What?' asked Lil E. What you mean RICO indictment? Most of them got away to Port Au Prince and--"

"Yea, lil nigga. You been so damn obsessed with finding your ole girl's killer, you neglected your own house! You fucked yourself! Got caught slippin'...her killer was right under your nose the whole time, lil nigga! You just too blind to see it!"

Lil E looked up, furious. "You?" he shouted, starting to reach for his gun.

Chapter Forty - Three

Kilo

"...and spin the block and park over there by the Waffle House until I call you to let you know it's safe to come and scoop us-" directed Jermaine as he used a speed loader to load the .223 green tips into the 100 round drum on his Kel-Tec PLR-16, which is a Mini-14 essentially, just an all carbon fiber version of the original.

"Bae, I got my own damn Glock on me," interrupted Jamie. "I'm coming with! I don't go to target practice every week at Gator Guns shooting range to be sitting in the fucking truck! "

Jermaine looked at the backseat, at his big brother, an exasperated look on his face at Jamie trying to butt-in on grown man shit. "You see what I gotta deal with?" asked Jay.

"What? My nigga-shit! I respect that shit!" Kilo said, laughing at his brother. "Shit, I'm really starting to like this girl- even if she is pigment challenged! " Kilo and Jamie both laughed together.

"'Thank you, Kian!" said Jamie, driving as fast as she could South on I-95 to get them to the tow truck impound lot where the newly acquired target, Lil E, was located at. "This boy caught himself tryna protect me from life! Boy-pulease! I am *not* some delicate lily flower! I can shoot two!"

Wow!" said Kilo, still laughing, "I like her more and more by the minute...

"Thank you again! There! It's settled then! I'm coming," stated Jamie, full of determination.

"No!" yelled Jay, getting angry at Kilo's interference. "You ain't coming!"

"C'mon, bruh. Let her come!" said Kilo.

"Bruh, let Isabella come-" started Jay.

"Bite your ma-fuckin' tongue!" said Kilo, interrupting, deadly serious now.

"Yea, just as I thought! Jamie, stay over by Waffle House..." said Jay, back to loading his drum.

Jamie just continued on driving and saying nothing as she drove, Kilo noticing the cute and mischievous smile on her pretty pink lips. Kilo knew she had no intention of staying put where Jay told her to. Kilo wasn't lying about coming around to like Jamie either. She had a lot of heart and Kilo really respected that. Plus, she seemed to genuinely love his brother, and that was a lot more important to him than the age difference or her being pigment challenged.

Putting those thoughts aside, Kilo got his head back in the game as they neared the Boynton Beach Boulevard exit on I-95, where the industrial area was located, the place they were headed to. Kilo put his four back-up magazines in his pockets and then fired off a text message.

Seconds later, Kilo checked his phone, which is on silent for their mission, and saw a received text from Haze. "Passing Lantana Road now-3 minutes bruh."

"Okay, make your first right onto Industrial Road..." said Jay, now they were exiting I-95 and heading West on Boynton Beach Boulevard.

Jamie then made the turn and followed the road around the bend and passed several different tow truck yards before seeing a big, near empty lot up ahead. She slowed her truck.

"That's it, right there, up ahead on the left," said Jay. "He's not alone either. I guess you was right that he knew about me and was setting me up...Okay, Jamie, let's drop bruh back 'round the back. Drop me off in front and go to Waffle House like I said."

"A'ight, let's do this...There goes Haze and da homies. Let's put in this work, bruh...."

Chapter Forty - Four

Detective Thomas Jones

"Yea, lil nigga. You been so obsessed with finding your old girl's killer, you neglected your own house! You fucked yourself! Got caught slippin'...Her killer was right under ya nose the whole time, nigga! You just too blind to see it!" said the new voice that Jones thought he might recognize, but wasn't sure about it. He could definitely sense the tension building up though.

"'You?!" shouted the voice he knew to be the teenage boy who had actually kidnapped him, even though things were looking worse for Jones. Even though it seemed that these visitors had the upper hand on his kidnapper, he had no doubt that his own outcome would hardly differ from the fate he would have had since he didn't have the answers to the questions he kept asking.

"Nah, lil nigga," said the visitor softly. "Of course it wasn't me. Nicole was like my own sister, and I wouldn't never do nothing that hurt her...But you out of line, and ...Well, you need to be put down before they catch you and bring da whole set down. You'll be with your old girl."

"So, if you ain't kill her-then who? I need to know..." said the kidnapper. Resigned.

"Her best friend...Skyla Hayworth..." replied the visitor.

"And who the fuck is that? Your smirk says you know, Uncle Grey..."

Jones blood went cold. Not only from hearing that Skyla had indeed killed Nicole Lewis, but also because the name Grey came immediately into the forefront of his mind, remembering the man who he had arrested for the murder of Weasel and his girlfriend in their bed after it had been made public about them being Jones' informants on the Southside of Lake Worth's crack trade almost two decades ago. Grey Goose had been found not guilty with the lack of physical evidence and then the sole witness having committed suicide. Shawn East was hung in his closet, but Jones knew that it had been no suicide. It had been Grey Goose. East had been murdered for being a rat as well.

Jones began to pull and rip all over again at his binds, now with a renewed vigor and determination, knowing what his fate will be if he doesn't free himself before this crazy conversation went any further south. Jones now knew what he was dealing with. He had put it all together after hearing them talk about Nicole, who was apparently his kidnapper's mother and Grey Goose-the visitor's 'sister'. She was Nicole Lewis, Jones' murder vic from the 12th Avenue store. This was seeming more and more crazy and complicated to him.

Once he had heard his girl, Skyla's name being mentioned as Nicole's killer, it took over his soul and almost stopped his heart. His heart was in his throat now because he was second-guessing himself. The whole world was coming crashing down on him and all he could do was think about the engagement ring he had been holding in his hand when he had been kidnapped.

Was the whole thing a setup from day one? he asked himself. Was Skyla just using his love for her to keep him from finding out about the murder she had committed on his watch? Jones found it hard to believe that the feelings they shared could be faked. Still making little progress on his duct-taped hands, he allowed his mind to wonder back to their conversation.

"Yea, lil nigga. Of course I know who she is...You sho' you wanna know?" Grey Goose asked Lil E.

"Tell me now! " the kidnapper demanded.

"Skyla Hayworth-she's your dad's wife. His *real* love and mother to his real kids..."

During the silence of that revelation, Jones looked up at the garage bay's windows and saw a big surprise. The face he saw in the window was that of Skyla- his future wife. It was real! he realized. But what was she doing here in the window, he asked himself. It didn't matter, because she was there for him...

Chapter Forty - Five

OG Haze, ZMA

Speeding down I-95 South, 110 miles an hour and trying to get to Boynton Beach as fast as they possibly could, Haze, Baby Boy and Glizzy were all strapped and ready to get to the work call. They had called the other homies and let them all know where to come, but they had already been on the road and only scooped up Glizzy along the way before jumping on I-95 and getting there as soon as they could.

"There they go, bruh," said Glizzy, directing Haze to the correct tow yard that he saw Jermaine and Kilo get dropped off at. Immediately afterwards, the white Jeep pulled off nonchalantly without raising any suspicion and then pulled up a block, pulling over to the side of the road.

"Okay, y'all, let's get this done with, load up..." said Haze, as he parked his truck and jumped out, staying low with his AR-15 with the 100 round drum-what was known as 'Micky Mouse Ears' in the hood. He started running towards the office after seeing Jermaine slide in like he owned the spot, wanting to get to the business faster.

Glizzy and Baby Boy went around back, following behind where they had seen Kilo run to. There was another car that pulled up as Haze slipped inside the glass front door to the office, but he just assumed that it was the rest of the ZMA members coming to put in work with them. He didn't even suspect who it really was.

Jermaine turned around fast and raised his big assault rifle, pointing it right at Haze before recognizing him and lowering his rifle. "Shit, my bad Big Homie. Shit, this nigga know me, so just fall

185

back till I get there and talk to him first. Just watch my back cause I don't know what he got on his mind in here, bruh, okay?" said Jermaine, making Haze uncomfortable.

"A'ight, bruh, but be careful. I'm right here and the other homies went round back to follow Kilo, so you covered. Let's just put in this work and go, before them laws come 'round lookin' fo' some smoke, a'ight?" said Haze.

"I gotcha, Big Homie..." Haze stayed back and peeked into the big garage bay that had been empty for a while, but that now had a man strapped to a chair in the middle and three men surrounding one boy, all having a conversation that Haze couldn't quite hear. He watched as Jermaine walked in, his gun brought up in firing position. "Bruh, y'all bout to be famous if y'all move an inch!" yelled Jay, getting the drop on the other dudes in the garage.

They all froze, weighing out all of their options in their heads individually. It was no longer a gang move, it was a self-preservation move now. Every man for himself. Haze knew the outcome would be sloppy, so he took cover behind the front desk, while still sticking his head and rifle barrel out on the ground next to the desk.

"What's this?" asked the big guy who Haze knew was that muthafucka, Grey Goose, from Haitian Sensations and Kraze Barye gang, 'Destroy the Barrier' from Taberre hood in Port Au Prince. Shit, Haze thought to himself, this just got very complicated, and he knew if they found out that ZMA was behind an attack on Haitian Sensations or Kraze Barye, it would cause an even bigger gang war. He knew that they couldn't let anyone leave this place alive or they would be responsible for a retaliatory attack on their own people.

"Bruh, y'all boys drop them fucking pee shooters or y'all finna be on da fuckin' news tonight!" yelled Jay in response.

186

They weighed their options, but then finally they realized that Jay was holding a fully automatic assault rifle with a drum. Not a lot of choice for them with their hand guns where accuracy could be a problem at that distance, as compared to Jay's advantage of being able to simply spray the whole area and wet all of them in one sweep. They made the right choice. They dropped their guns and looked at Lil E. "This is your work?" Grey Goose asked him.

"'Y'all niggas thought I need you? Shit, y'all needed *me*! I told you that, Grey!" screamed Lil E, overconfident at Jay's protection and enforcement, having the ups on his newly declared enemies.

"And who the fuck is this lil kid, huh? Your lil brother, I assume?" said Grey Goose, baiting his trap.

"Nah, nigga. This my homie," said Lil E, pulling out his Desert Eagle .45 only to place it against Grey Goose's head and pull the trigger.

Brains and skull fragments splashed all over the other two guys with Grey Goose and they were immediately blinded but still dove for the floor, trying to retrieve their weapons. They both fell down and wiped the blood out of their eyes, reaching for their respective guns and trying to get control of an out of hand situation.

Just then, the back door bursted open and in came Kilo, Baby Boy and Glizzy, all having their guns in the upright, firing position. "Don't fucking try it," said Kilo, firing one round next to the big dude on the floor covered in brains and trying to bring his gun up towards Jermaine. He paused. It was like the whole garage was frozen. Nobody made a move and everyone was stone still.

"So," said Lil E. "Your moms killed my moms?"

"Your moms killed my pops! " Jermaine said in anger.

"Fool, I don't care nothing about your pops! I only care about my ole girl, nigga!" said Lil E, bringing his Desert Eagle into a firing position, only to be shot before he could get there.

Haze saw what was coming and saw that the other homies' attention was all on the two men on the floor who had just been trying to reach for their guns, so Haze took the shot. Haze fired one shot and clipped Lil E in the shoulder holding his Desert Eagle and then he immediately fired two more rounds as Lil E turned away and quickly took off running-no-sprinting, as fast as he could, toward a side door that they hadn't noticed there before.

Seeing that his next two shots had missed, Haze started firing in a quick succession until Lil E had made it out of that side door. Just as Haze stopped firing, he noticed that more shots had joined his toward that side door and in all the confusion, while Glizzy and Baby Boy were putting bullets in the heads of the two men on the ground, two women had suddenly burst into the back door and began to chase after that boy who had run out of the side door they had just been firing at.

Haze jumped up and looked toward Kilo, who began screaming for the women to stop.

"Mom! Stop! Just leave that shit alone, we got this!" yelled Kilo.

"Skyla! Come here!" said the Detective that was still taped to the chair. Baby Boy lifted his gun in order to shoot Jones in the head but was stopped by Skyla's scream.

"NOOO!" screamed Skyla, forgetting about chasing after Lil E and running back towards Jones. She ran over to him and immediately began taking off the tape and trying to free him from the restraints.

Baby boy saw her reaction and stood down, thoroughly confused.

Chapter Forty - Six

Skyla

Skyla had just seen Red. She saw the boy who had apparently started all of this drama and kidnapped her man, and he was about to get away. She just reacted. She started firing from the gun that Kilo had given her back after killing Sin and all that drama had passed.

"Moms! Stop..." she heard her son yelling for her to stop, but then through her brain came the voice of her lover, her future husband, her fiancé. She heard Tommy's voice. He was calling for help. "Skyla! Come here!" yelled Jones. He needed her help.

Just that quickly, she forgot all about chasing that boy who had started all of this and she turned around. Seeing that a man was pointing a big gun at her man, she immediately reacted. "NOOOO!" she screamed.. She didn't care about the boy anymore, or any of this drama anymore. It was all second to what she was seeing and she had to stop Tommy from getting hurt. She ran over, and pushing back at the man with the gun, she pulled out the taser needles and started loosening Jones' arms and legs from the straps that were confining him. "It's okay, baby! I got you!" she mumbled as she helped him to get up and out of that nasty chair. He was severely beaten and in a lot of pain. He was also covered in blood and smelled of feces and urine. He has obviously been tortured.

She helped him along as she saw her sons and a few of the men running out the side door and chasing after the boy who had gotten away in all the confusion. Skyla was crying, shocked at Jones' appearance and couldn't get over the fact that she had almost lost him like she had lost Maniac a few years ago. "I'm sorry, baby! Are you okay? I couldn't just wait on them to come get you for me, I had to make sure you were okay, baby," said Skyla, crying and barely able to control her hysteria.

"I tho-I thought that it wasn't real. I tho-I thought that you didn't care..." Jones mumbled through all of his pain. He was barely able to talk as he was shaking and crying.

"No! Of course not, baby! I had to come get you! I love you! Of course I couldn't leave you alone!" said Skyla, hearing tires of vehicles taking off.

SCCCCRRRRRTTTTT!!!

There were some more cars that followed. The boys were going after the kidnapper. She hoped they got his ass. She hoped they killed him for what he did to her Tommy. "I found the ring, Thomas..." said Skyla sadly.

"Yea, baby. I was going to ask you when you got there. I had that ring for over week now and just didn't know how to ask. I was just about to ask you when-when that kid knocked on my window asking for help..." said Jones.

"Let's get you to a hospital, It's okay now, baby," said Skyla, reassuringly.

"Damn, this is a crazy day...I don't know how I'm going to explain this one. How I am going to cover up what you did to Nicole Lewis, but don't worry, I'll figure it out..."

Chapter Forty - Seven

Lil E

He was shot bad and he was bleeding even worse, but he couldn't stop now. He knew that they were on his ass. How the fuck did he miss this? he asked himself. How the fuck did he not see this shit coming? When he saw that Jermaine had showed up, he was hopeful because he was being saved from Grey Goose and what he had planned for him. But then it set the scene where he would be dead either way. It looked as if Jermaine had figured out about him before he had figured out about Jermaine. He had somehow missed it, slipping.

He was speeding as fast as his little Ford Maverick could go, he had jumped on I-95 going South. Back to Miami. Back to Lil Haiti. A place that he knew and that the people knew him and a place where he could control the outcome and could fight back. He had lost his phone and couldn't even call for any backup to help him. Ain't this bout a bitch? he asked himself another time. He had got caught slippin'. After all the shit his ole girl had given him about being on point, here he was. Caught off guard.

"FUCK!" he yelled, trying to hold his shoulder with one hand while steering the truck with his left. He was driving recklessly but he knew they were gaining on him. His 'brothers'. He had figured it all out with what Grey Goose had disdainfully said, "And who the fuck is this lil kid, huh? Your lil brother, I assume?"

That had told it all. His father was also their father. His mother had been messing with their father and had gotten pregnant from him. Sounds like something his mother would do, to be so overly confident in herself that she never even considered that he might choose his wife over her. "FUCK!" he screamed again. How the fuck did she not tell him? Why would she keep such a secret from him? he wondered. Embarrassment. Pain. Shame. He knew why. It all made sense. She had probably been in love with him and yet he had chosen to remain with his wife and his family, he couldn't believe this shit.

He was starting to lose control of his truck, it was like he was fading, in and out. He was thinking so hard that the blood he was losing was really affecting his judgement. A Cadillac SUV moved right into his path as he was going 100 miles an hour. He swerved to go around but rammed into another truck as if it was standing still. It only slowed him down some, but when he hit the gas again, his tough little Ford truck responded instantly.

He looked into the rearview mirror and saw the truck he had hit as it ran off the highway and onto the median, crashing into the guard rail, totaling the truck, and most likely seriously hurting the driver. Lil E didn't give a fuck at this point. He was more worried about the little car that was barreling down on him.

He stood on the gas pedal and swerved around some big tractor trailers that were all in the middle lane as he passed Boca Raton's Glades Road exit, almost entering into Broward County. He again swerved around the next one as an idea came into his mind. He was watching as the little Japanese car was still on his trail and how it was being expertly maneuvered around all of the obstacles and avoiding all the other drivers on the busy highway. He had a trick for that, though. Something to leave them soaking wet. Dead. Suddenly, something surprised him, though. He heard, and even felt the bullets striking his truck. "FUCK!" he said for the third time, starting to feel weak and his eyesight started to fade away.

In the rearview mirror, he saw his homie, his 'friend', and his actual little brother, shooting at his tires as he leans out of the passenger window of the car they were chasing him in. He only had one last play, and he intended it to work, or he would most certainly die.

As he came up on the next tractor trailer in the long line of the busy I-95 traffic, he swerved right in front of it and hit his emergency brakes, causing a huge cloud of tire smoke and scared the truck driver into stomping on his own air brakes. The tractor trailer immediately jack-knifed and blocked the whole five lanes of I-95, including Jay and his brother-Lil E's other brother.

Lil E had tried to regain control of his truck but couldn't seem to disengage the parking brake that he had hit in order to control his slide into the drift to cause the whole traffic block.

He whipped his wheel around and tried to set his truck straight but only made it about a quarter of a mile before losing all control of his vehicle. The truck flipped over and over and over again as he was thrown around the truck's cab like a rag doll and finally out through a broken window as he had not had his seatbelt on. The last thing Lil E saw was his mother and father walking hand in hand down the center lane of I-95 toward him, trying to save him, trying to bring him home. He smiled to himself. He was coming home, he thought... then his eyes closed, and he thought no more.

Chapter Forty - Eight

Kilo

Kilo couldn't believe it, Jermaine had actually hit one of that lil nigga's tires and he was swerving out of control. He was excited, now they had him. But his thoughts of victory were quickly put down as the tractor trailer in front of him swerved and jack- knifed in the middle of I-95, causing the cars ahead of him to swerve and stop suddenly.

He hit the brakes in his mom's old Toyota Camry. He looked to make sure that his brother was okay. He saw him breathing hard but not hurt. He looked around and as he did, he heard the sirens. "Damn, bruh. Sirens. We got to get the fuck outta here..." said Kilo, looking in the rearview and backing the car up until he was on the shoulder of I-95 and reversing the car just enough to get the car even with the exit ramp for Atlantic Boulevard, the Pompano exit in Broward County.

He slowly maneuvered the car onto the ramp and carefully got up the ramp, so that he didn't draw attention, but would look like any other traveler that was trying to avoid the dead stand-still traffic on the highway, a common occurrence in South Florida. Nobody even seemed to notice. He crept along, while looking up ahead at the flipped over Ford truck and seeing no movement, he was tempted to go down there and finish that kid once and for all. Something stopped him though. As he awaited the red light at the top of the off ramp, he saw the flames from the under-carriage start to spread. Then suddenly, the flames spread to the gas tank that exploded, almost like a bomb.

BOOOOM!

The whole truck was engulfed in flames. The truck lifted 5 feet off of the road when it exploded. It was no small explosion. The gas tank had to have been on full for it to have had such a big explosion like that, thought Kilo.

"Well," said Kilo quietly. "I guess that's that then. That is the end of 'Aunt Nikki' and her family line, right?"

"I guess so," said Jermaine sadly.

Kilo made the left turn toward the beach side when the red light turned green. They were silent for a few moments, both watching their trail to make sure nobody had reported them to the police for them shooting out of the car at the truck and causing the big explosion in the middle of I-95 during rush hour traffic. Kilo saw in his rearview mirror that they weren't being followed.

"Why do you sound like that?" asked Kilo, curiously.

"Fooly, I ain't on nothing, bruh. It's all good, no worries. I'm just wondering what the homies are doing with that cop that was all tied up back there..."

"Shit! My Phone!" said Kilo. "I left my phone in Jamie's truck...who by the way is a real one. I'll say that any day of the week, bruh. She came back for you, my nigga."

"Yea. After I told her not to."

"That's the very definition of a 'real one', my nigga. She did what needed to be done and fuck the consequence or what anybody else told her to do. She is a real one. She did bring mom here, though. So, she *is* in trouble for that one..." Kilo said, laughing now that the moment had passed and they could let the adrenaline out of their systems, the stress of the gunfight now behind them.

"Don't worry about your friend, my Z. It was either him or us, bruh. You did what you had to do, my nigga. That's how this shit works, bruh. You take a life and save a life. Our ole girl would've never let us live if we had left that cop to die. Plus, once that lil nigga found out what she did to Aunt Nikki, he would have come for her anyways. Better to handle that shit now and get it out the way. Now it's smooth sailing from here on out. Beef been cooked and it's time to eat desert...the fruits of our labor..."

"Yea, I know, Kian. It just wasn't what I...it just ain't go how I thought it would. It's all good though. At least mom and you are safe, and Jamie ain't get hurt... that girl, shit," said Jermaine wincing.

"It's okay, lil bruh. Just let it go, bruh. It's all gon' be okay man..."

Stopping at the Metro PCS store, Kilo bought a burner phone, so they could call the homies and make sure everything was cool back in Boynton Beach and that everyone had gotten away. After talking to Jamie, who was the only phone number that they could remember by heart to call.

"Yea, we good. We back to your mama house, so just get back over here and make sure you clean when you do. The cop is trying to figure out how he is going to explain all of this shit. So, get back here now, okay? Love you..." said Jamie, not knowing she was on speaker phone.

Jermaine blushed, never one for public display of affection, especially in front of his big brother, but still mumbled 'love you too' back to her.

Chapter Forty - Nine

Detective Jones

Jones got out of the bathtub after spending a good amount of time in there while trying to wash off all of the agony and fear that he had suffered through, as well as the grime that had accumulated from being physically abused and tortured. He had argued with Skyla for a full 10 minutes as they arrived at JFK hospital about him not wanting to go and get medical help. He was adamant about not going that route being that the police would then be summoned to investigate and he couldn't afford that before they had all got together and got their stories straight.

He had been so full of fear as he sat in that chair, but not because of the fear of dying. It was the fear that Skyla had only been using him and never had loved him as he loved her. That would have been unbearable and he would have rather died than face that sort of reality anyways.

So, once he had seen her face in that window, it gave him, not only the will to live, but also it gave him the motivation to make sure that he protected her from what she had done. He was a Homicide detective, so he believed that all life was precious. But he was also in love with this woman and couldn't arrest her or allow her to be arrested.

In the movies, he was sure that the Detective in his position would do the right thing and put her away. He might even be there for her while she was away. Not Jones. He would cover for her without question, he would lie and kill for her. He would do whatever needed to be done so that she wouldn't have to ever face that fate. He knew why she had done it. Sure. He had figured it all out after hearing all the conversations before all of the bullets

197

started flying everywhere. Yea, he told himself, he could understand her killing the person behind her husband's murder. That was something that he could definitely understand. He would have done the same if that had happened to him. He would kill or die for her. He loved her that much. He was in love with her, no doubt. She would be his wife, now that all of this was going to be behind them.

Getting dressed, he ordered an Uber and told her to allow him to go into the station by himself. He knew how to appeal to Captain Reider's sense of loyalty to his men. He would be as vague as he possibly could and he would redirect any investigation into the dead men on the floor in that tow yard's office. Grey Goose and his men were Haitian Sensations. He would bury the whole thing under the guise of their kidnapping him for reasons unknown. It would work. It would have to.

He heard the beep of the horn in front of Skyla's house.

"Okay, baby. I will be back when this is all cleared up. Wish me luck..." he said before walking out. "Cause I'm definitely going to need all the luck I can get.."

Chapter Fifty

"Quan, you have nothing to apologize for, it's my fault-"

"No. It isn't. That's what I wanted to tell you. I know I let my own mind get out of hand, but I realize now that it's just not meant to be and you don't owe me anything. You did nothing wrong. It was all in my head and I want you to know that that cop...well, he is a very lucky man to have you."

"Thank you, Quan-" replied Skyla.

"And he better treat you right," said Quan, interrupting. "But, I guess I kind of know he will. That's why you chose him. I just want you to be happy, Sky..."

"Thank you, Quan," she said. "Oh, and Quan? I am."

She watched as Quan turned and walked off. She felt bad but she knew it was neither one of their fault, it was just the universe and how it works. She was glad that her son had a best friend like Quan though. He had saved her son twice and rode with her on her drug addiction, trying to get rehabilitated and so much more. He would always be a part of their family. She knew he would always be there for them, and she was grateful for him.

Just as she was about to call him again, she saw Tommy Jones walk into their backyard, limping still. Her whole face lit up. She ran up to him and jumped into his arms, temporarily forgetting about his injuries in her excitement. She hugged and kissed him all over his battered face, before he finally called to Jay and Kian. "Give me a moment, baby..." he said and then walked over to Jermaine and Kian, speaking to them momentarily.

She noticed that he didn't want to push too hard with a hug, but after a few moments of speaking, thanking them, she thought, he shook both of their hands and then walked back over to her.

"Baby, what was that-" she started to ask him.

He bent down onto his painfully hurt knee and brought out the ring out of his pocket.

"Bae-what-are...Oh, my God! Are you-Is this?" stuttered Skyla.

"Woman, I am not a full circle without you. You make me whole and fill my empty heart. I want to spend the rest of my life with you-if you'll have me. Skyla? Will you marry-" said Jones before Skyla pulled him to his feet excitedly hugging and kissing him all over.

"Yes! Yes, baby! Of course I will! I love you so much Tommy! Yes!" she said and continued her assault on his face with her pretty lips.

Jermaine and Kilo both started clapping as Imani ran up and jumped into Jones' arms, happily hugging him and accepting him as her stepfather, already having spent so much time with him.

Things were looking very hopeful for the whole ZMA Family. Everyone in the backyard was smiling and laughing. Everyone was celebrating and happy. That is, until Jones' phone beeped, with a text message coming in. "Oh, shit," said Jones, looking down at his offending phone. "This isn't good. Looks like we have a problem."

Epilogue

Lil E

Being thrown from his truck and damn near killed didn't stop Lil E. He felt indestructible. He was hurting bad. He felt like he might die. But the pure anger and hatred flowing through his veins and pumping through his soul kept him going. Revenge. He had been unconscious apparently, but he was up and in some bushes on the fence line of the I-95 exit. He had been thrown from the vehicle, he figured.

As he looked down the highway and saw a big plume of black smoke, burning fuel, he assumed, he was glad that he was thrown from his vehicle. He was alive. He wouldn't have been alive if he *had* been wearing his seatbelt and wasn't thrown from the truck. But another good thing was the little Japanese car had not followed. That meant that they thought him to be dead and still among the remains in the truck.

"Wishful thinking," he said to himself. They had not killed him. But he knew that if he didn't get away from here fast, he would either be dead or incarcerated. So, he crawled towards the fence and pulled himself up to his feet. He began to climb the fence and winced as the pain overtook him and overwhelmed his being again, almost making him pass out at the mere motion in his bullet wounded arm and shoulder.

He finally threw himself over the six foot fence and started moving carefully through the dense bushes and trees that lined the highway as a sound breaker. He moved by holding onto the trees and leaning on them. He eventually heard all of the Police moving around on the side of the highway. Probably looking for any evidence or survivors. They didn't know about the shooting yet, but once they did, it would be really bad. It would cause them to start doing checkpoints and possibly bring out the dogs if they knew the driver of that truck had gotten away. He moved even faster and tried to put as much distance in between him and the scene as he possibly could. He is on his own now, that much he knew. He had nowhere to go. He could only think of one place where he could stay hidden from the investigation that Grey Goose had hinted about. He knew he had to be careful. But, knowing how she felt about him, he was sure he could go to her and she would do everything she could to bring him into her family and protect him. He had to go back to Tasha. To the Jamaicans.

Once this passed and he got back on his feet, Lil E would come back and strike again. Lil E wouldn't let this shit slide, he knew what had to be done. He knew that he would do it. This wasn't over, but he had the advantage now. They thought that he was dead. He would use that to his advantage and let them fall into being complacent. Let them think he was dead and no longer a threat to them. That was when he would strike and then he would have his Revenge, then they would feel the Razor's Double Edge of Revenge. They would feel what he feels. For they all knew Revenge was a meal best served cold, and nobody was colder than Lil E.

Stay Tuned!

A Razor's Edge of Revenge III: A Final Cut

www.freetaboopublishing.com

Free Taboo Publishing, LLC. presents

A VICTIM *of* JUSTICE

BOOK CLUB
QUESTIONS

TABOO

Free Taboo Publishing LLC, presents

A VICTIM IN
THUG
MANSION

PARENTAL ADVISORY
EXPLICIT CONTENT

TABOO

FREE TABOO PUBLISHING, LLC,
PRESENTS
__ A BOOK TO KEEP TEENS FROM THE WRONG PATH __

A MESSAGE TO MY TEENAGE SELF

BRIAN MICKO YEARY

About the Author

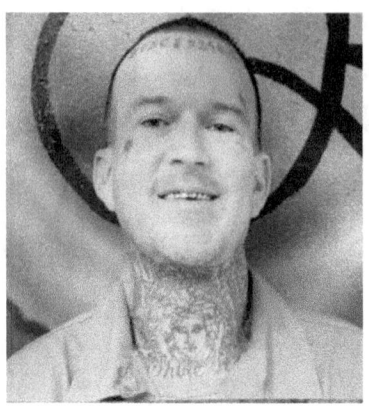

Taboo, or Brian Micko Yeary, is a Federal Prisoner who has been sentenced to die in prison for non-violent, victimless gun and drug possessions charges. Being an advocate for Criminal Justice Reform and while waiting for retroactivity to apply the First Step Act to his stacked 924(c) sentences, Taboo started FREE TABOO PUBLISHING, LLC to bring attention not only to his own situation, but to also help to publish other talented authors and poets who are also Victims of Justice incarcerated in this criminal INjustice system.

Sentenced to 91 years for a draconian 924(c) sentencing enhancement that has since been corrected by Congress, Taboo still sits under this unfair and ridiculous sentence. Convinced by Tom Cotton of Arkansas, Congress decided that the 924(c) law is only unfair to those who were sentenced AFTER 2018 and not those who are actually still suffering right now from the unfairness of it, so they withheld retroactivity from older cases sentenced before the First Step Act.

Most convicts in Taboo's position would become a product of their environment in a Maximum Security Penitentiary overrun by gangs and violence, but this author instead persevered and established FREE TABOO PUBLISHING in April 2022 and introduced his debut novel, "A Victim of Justice" shortly thereafter. He has two new authors to introduce and a trilogy of his own coming out soon. He lives in Lee County US Penitentiary with no cats, dogs, yet a lot of hope in Congress to pass legislation for retroactivity and equality in sentencing reform.